Kristin O'Donnell Tubb

SELLING HOPE

A FEIWEL AND FRIENDS BOOK
An Imprint of Macmillan

Library of Congress Cataloging-in-Publication Data

Tubb, Kristin O'Donnell.
Selling hope / Kristin O'Donnell Tubb. — 1st ed.
p. cm.
Summary: In 1910, just before the earth passes through the tail of Halley's
Comet, thirteen-year-old Hope McDaniels, whose father is a magician in a
traveling vaudeville show, tries to earn enough money to quit the circuit by selling
"anti-comet pills," with the help of fellow performer Buster Keaton.
ISBN: 978-0-312-61122-4
1. Vaudeville—Fiction. 2. Magic tricks—Fiction. 3. Halley's comet—
Fiction. 4. Hoaxes—Fiction. 5. Single-parent families—Fiction.
6. Mothers—Fiction.] I. Title.
PZ7.T796Se 2010
[Fic]—dc22
2010012571

Book design by Michelle McMillian

Feiwel and Friends logo designed by Filomena Tuosto

First Edition: 2010

10 9 8 7 6 5 4 3 2 1

www.feiwelandfriends.com

For Mom & Dad, who happen to know
a thing or two about hope

May 1, 1910

SEVENTEEN DAYS
till the End of the World.

NEWS HEADLINE

*Earth Will Pass Through Comet's 24-Million-Mile-Long
Tail on May 18*

ross-Eyed Jane poked her head into the tent. Her kinky
yellow hair puffed in after her.

"We gots fifteen more minutes with the tarot cards before
she and Nick go on." Cross-Eyed Jane addressed me as "she,"
even when she was talking directly to me. This, coupled with
the fact that she was cross-eyed, often made it difficult to know
who Jane was talking about. But I was the only other person
in the tent, so I assumed her "she" was me. I smiled.

Jane smiled back, her wrinkled face carving into deep ruts,
and gazed over my shoulder. I moved my head up and to the
left to where I thought she was looking, but those crawly eyes
of hers crept right past me. Erm . . . *left* past me.

I'm tellin' ya, the old gal was so cross-eyed,
when she rolled her eyes, she hit her ears!

Huck. There it was—the surest sign that I needed to leave this vaudeville circuit once and for all: those awful wisecracks. I guess everyone has a little voice inside his or her head, pointing out all of the things that are funny and fantastical and odd. But *my* internal voice? Equipped with the kind of one-liner jokes that made vaudeville famous. Not exactly the conscience of your average thirteen-year-old.

I adjusted my robes, the ones I had "borrowed" from the costume trunk, so I'd look more like a true medium. The robes were crafted of a thick red tapestry and weighed upward of twenty pounds. It took half my strength just to keep them draped across my tiny frame. But the robes added an air of mystery to our booth, accented by the massive candles, which threw skipping yellow light across the canvas walls, dripping colorful wax on the dusty ground beneath. Did I know how to put on a show! I should—I'd learned from the best.

Jane and I had set up shop—and by *shop,* I mean our little canvas booth—next to the other peddlers, just outside the vaudeville theater in Des Moines, Iowa, our latest tour stop. There was a row of us who made a little extra green that way. The actors and stagehands peddled everything from sheet music to medicinal elixirs to stuff they'd purchased in the last town, plus 20 percent. The theatergoers loved this makeshift storefront; for them it was part of the vaudeville experience. And too, Mr. Whitting and the other managers took a healthy cut of our profits, so they saw our little side businesses as just fine and dandy.

"Lead the first Coin in," I whispered to Cross-Eyed Jane. She clicked her tongue at me; she hated it when I called them that. I began to hum, quietly at first, then letting it grow into a noisy, low moan. I told myself I was getting into character. Plus, the moaning sounded good to the Coins. That's what I called our customers—the Coins.

Hummmmmmmm. Farewell, Hope McDaniels. Greetings to Mademoiselle Ari, Gifted Child Medium and Foreseer of the Future.

Cross-Eyed Jane ducked out of the smallish tent, then back in again, goading a female Coin before her. Jane cupped her hand about the Coin's elbow, trying to lead her to the table where I sat. The Coin yanked her arm from Jane's grip and shot her a look of utter disgust, as if she might somehow contract Jane's crazy eye "disease." This particular Coin was so big, she almost knocked over three of my candles entering our booth.

I'm not sayin' the gal was overweight, but she was plump in places where most folks don't have places!

Jane jutted her chin at me. "That's her," she whispered to the Coin. "She's young, doncha know, but her youth allows her channels to be fully open to the future." Jane tried winking her spacey eye at me, but it appeared as if she were winking at the heavens instead. I cleared my throat to stifle a giggle. That "open channels" bit always got me.

I had to hand it to Jane. When she came up with this idea of a "child medium," I was skeptical. Adults forking over a jitney

3

to hear a thirteen-year-old talk about money and love and death? Most of the adults I knew didn't even pause to hear me discuss the weather, much less pay an entire nickel to hear it. But Jane was right—the Coins loved me. I relaxed them, as though I was simply peeking ahead in a lighthearted parlor game of Ouija board, as though I couldn't possibly be the bearer of bad news. And I must admit, I loved the power that came with telling adults what they should worry about.

Our partnership was a good one, mine and Jane's. I asked her once why she didn't just read the cards herself and keep all the money, instead of just half. She'd snorted, she'd laughed so hard.

"Me, read fortunes?" she'd said with a cough. "People want to see their futures as fresh and lively, like Hope, lassie. A withered old grouch like me don't exactly set the proper backdrop for a prosperous road ahead, eh?"

Yes, Jane was no spring chicken. She was so old, she looked like she gave her pallbearers the slip!

Jane and I split all money fifty-fifty. And there was nothing like having a wad of cash stashed in your grouch bag. Because I would never—_never_—not have money again.

Jane now folded herself out of the tent, and the Coin she'd procured perched on the caned chair opposite me. Her knees wouldn't fit under the tiny folding table between us, so she sat sidewise. I began flipping tarot cards onto the shimmery tablecloth, placing the worn papers into a large, deliberate cross. The middle of the cross I left bare, for the moment. I'd come to

4

discover that flipping that middle card is the Grande Finale and should be coaxed slowly. *Coax* and *hoax* rhyme. Huh.

The pips that I turned for this Coin were all minor characters, like The Page and The Queen. What. A. Bore.

"Mmm. Mmm-hmm," I muttered, and nodded knowingly. The Coin shifted, and the tiny chair moaned. I flipped another card: Judgment.

"Oh!" I said. The Coin gasped.

Did I mention? I didn't know the first thing about reading tarot cards. The cards themselves were beautiful—blues and purples and reds and oranges that swirled and twined in inky vines, taking forms such as The Empress and The Hanged Man and Death. Each card was a masterpiece. The worn, beloved deck belonged to Cross-Eyed Jane, but she always said, "Lovey, these cards tells me they belong to *her*." (That would be me.) When I was ten, she'd allow me to play with them like they were paper dolls. Now I played with them for money.

Next from the deck: The Magician. One of my least favorite cards, not because my father was a magician, but because his love of magic rendered me essentially homeless. I groaned.

The Coin's eyes grew wide. "What is it?"

The cross of cards was complete, except for that final middle card. Now for The Show.

I placed the remainder of the cards on the edge of the table. Then I rubbed my hands together and blew on them, as if they were icy cold. I swirled my hands mere inches above the incomplete cross, feeling their energy. The Coin ate up this hooey like, well . . . apparently like she ate up *everything*: with gusto.

"You are . . ." I closed my eyes for a moment. "Unhappy."

The Coin nodded.

Zing. Well, honestly, that one was common sense. The only people who went to a medium were unhappy people. I always started with that one, and I always got it right.

I narrowed my eyes and studied my Coin. Wedding ring, decent clothes, furrowed brow. Pretty, in a plump sort of way.

"You're worried about something."

The Coin nodded again. She leaned forward in the tiny chair, and her brown eyes widened. She apparently thought I was on to something.

"You're worried about your marriage."

But the Coin shook her head and her shoulders slumped ever so slightly. I knew I'd guessed incorrectly before she even spoke. "No. No, I have a wonderful husband."

"Yes, yes, of course. You're worried about money." Always the next one I tried.

The Coin shook her head again, more fervently this time. Her eyes blazed, and her face screwed up like a twisted dish towel. "No, money's not an issue, you imp!" she shouted, and pounded the table with the palm of her hand. "I knew this was a waste of my time!"

Money's not an issue? Fancy that! Money's an issue for everyone, lady. I felt a little flame of anger ignite inside me at this sudden turn. No money problems! Pah!

But I needed this nickel. "You're worried about . . . ," I continued. My hands hovered over the bland cards that this Coin received for her reading. I wasn't quite sure what to try next. Awful marriages and money problems covered almost everyone. "You're worried about . . . your health."

The Coin drooped in her chair, and I thought for sure that I'd lost her, that she'd had enough of this hoax. But she surprised me. "Yes," she whispered into her lap. "Is it going to kill us all?"

My mind whirred. It? Kill us all? The only thing that could be was . . .

"Halley's Comet?"

"Yes!" The Coin bolted upright and gripped my wrists so tightly my skin turned white beneath her fingers.

"Let go, please." I said it softly, so as not to alarm Cross-Eyed Jane, who might very well enter the tent with a cocked pistol if she thought I was in danger. The Coin tightened her grip, her fingernails piercing my skin. Her eyes shifted between my face and the cards sprawled on the table between us, and there was a black spot of—fear?—that hadn't been there before. My heart raced like a locomotive.

"Are we all going to die?" she said. "Will the poisonous gasses suffocate us? Will the comet ram into our world? Why, the impact alone would . . ."

I shook my head in disbelief, wriggling to free myself from her grasp. Sure, I knew Earth was going to travel through the tail of Halley's Comet later this month; everyone had been talking about it since the turn of the new year. But kill us? Pah! The newspapers said the world's top scientists didn't believe that, so neither did I.

This Coin is such the fool! What a shame I'm not a mind reader. I could charge her half price.

7

I freed myself quickly from her grip. My "real job" as a magician's assistant required me to don handcuffs quite often. That rarely had its benefits, but this was indeed one of those times.

My wrists were tender to the touch, perhaps bruised. I rotated them in circles to regain feeling in my fingers.

The Coin had commenced to gripping the edge of the table and swaying to and fro in the tiny, groaning chair. I picked up the deck of cards and shuffled through them in my lap, hand-selecting the Grande Finale card:

The World.

I flipped it into the center of the X and widened my eyes like I truly saw death and destruction in this Coin's future. "It's—it's . . . too black! Too black! No light! *I . . . can't . . . breathe!*" I raised my hands to my throat, gagging and choking and making an all-too-obvious spectacle of myself.

The Coin leapt to her feet, toppling the table of cards and kicking aside the tiny chair. She shoved her way under the wall of the tent, rather than ducking through its flap, and dragged down two burning candles in the process. Blazing candles touched dry canvas and the tent ignited. Flames were soon eating our booth from the bottom up.

I had one pitcher of water, which I threw on the fire, dousing part of the blaze.

"Jane!" I yelled. "Water! Quick!"

Cross-Eyed Jane came in but moments later with a bucket of water, and the fire was soon nothing but a steaming pile of wet, reeking canvas. I was shaking, partly the result of being so near a large fire, and partly the result of having to defend my-self against this unstable Coin.

"Lovey! She's all right?"

I had a gaping hole in my booth caused by a desperate Coin who thought the world was going to end in seventeen days, and my funds would be largely depleted after I paid Jane for the damages. I lived in teeny railroad cars and shabby boardinghouses scattered about the country, and my best friend was a fifty-two-year-old cross-eyed gypsy. I wore twenty-pound robes that stank like smoke, and now my father needed my help performing magic tricks, a feat that he believed might allow him to someday change the course of the world. Honestly, he believed his sleight of hand was a gift that could unite the masses. Illusion or *dis*illusion? You tell me.

I threw off my charred costume, revealing the next cos-tume underneath.

"I'm the candy, Jane. Really," I sighed. "Does Nick need me onstage yet?"

I loved backstage. It was quiet, except for the occasional burst of howling laughter from the audience that penetrated the lush, velvety curtains. Stagehands rushed on tiptoe and communi-cated with gestures and pointing. The illumination was second-hand, provided solely by the few rays of light that bent around corners from the searing-hot stage. If only the entire world were like this—muffled and dark and once removed.

I had this little routine that I conducted before I went onstage. I didn't do it for good luck nor to ensure a good performance.

No, I did it so I could remember the things I felt I was in danger of forgetting.

I unfolded the square of red flannel and rubbed it against my cheek. It was gritty, not as soft as it once had been. Likely from years of absorbing apologies.

"I'm sorry, Mama," I whispered into it. "I'm sorry I couldn't do more."

I smelled the flannel, too. It smelled like . . . well, grubby fabric. Still, I imagined I smelled my mother in there. I do not remember what she smelled like.

I worried about this, but Cross-Eyed Jane assured me that I would be a marvel if I remembered anything about her. I was only eight when she died. Nick never discussed her. Never. I had a gritty red square of quilting fabric that was hers. Everything else was pawned before we left. One must travel light on the vaudeville circuit.

Speaking of traveling light, did you hear the one about the boy who did just that? All he packed was kerosene and matches!

Oh, thank you, folks. Thank you. No applause, please. Just throw money.

Standing onstage was akin to standing in a box of sun: bright, hot, and full of squint and sweat. Beyond the perimeter of the stage dwelled the murky outline of the heads of the audience members. I stood next to my father in a pose that, if it were struck anywhere but a magic act, would be beyond odd:

one arm lifted in the air, one arm outstretched toward the shenanigans, one toe pointed forward—a deranged ballerina. Absurd.

I suppose there is no need to underscore the fact that I was not a performer at heart.

My father, however . . . his eyes were shut and his fists were balled and raised to the heavens, as if he were gripping the air above his golden head. Nick was more alive here than anywhere else on the planet. Not *here,* as in Des Moines, Iowa, but up here, in the box of sun.

"If you live in doubt and fear," Nick was saying. He tucked his hand behind the lapel of his jacket and rummaged around for his prop. While so doing, he shot me a quick wink. I smiled. I actually liked this bit; it was one of the few acts in which I was little more than another of his props—and, yes, being a prop was fine by me. It beat the alternative, by which I mean taking an active role.

"If you dwell in a state of constant fear and dread . . ." Nick was having some trouble with this trick. He fumbled around inside the breastplate of his jacket until . . . yes!

He pulled an object from his jacket. The audience strained to see it. It was . . . it was . . .

A snake!

"If you cannot break free from the shackles of fear and dread, you contribute naught! You bite and suck but give nothing! You are a drain on the kingdom!" He steered the black snake deftly toward the front row of attendees, and it hissed as if on cue. Wheesh. Nick was on fire tonight.

"But . . ." Nick jabbed the air with his finger, and his voice dropped to a near-whisper. The audience took its cue and hushed itself after the excitement of the snake. "If you accept goodness and light into your life . . ." I handed him a folded newspaper, which he flipped open with his left hand while still gripping the snake with his right. He gently wrapped the snake in newspaper and placed it on the table in front of him as if it were frankincense and myrrh.

"If you yearn for justice . . . ," Nick said.

Then he pulled a tattered book from—*where?* The audience murmured at this point, as they always did. *Had that book been behind him the whole time?*

A book. That was new. He usually used a brick in this bit.

Nick raised the book above his head, the title *Leaves of Grass* facing out toward the crowd. *Leaves of Grass* by Walt Whitman, a poet, philosopher, and the reason why Nick believed that a two-bit magician and his daughter plodding about the country could alter the cosmos. "Alter the cosmos"—Nick's words, not mine. Well, Walt Whitman's words, actually.

"You. Can. *Transform!*"

At that, Nick slammed the text down onto the newspaper. The crowd shrieked. He then lifted the book and placed it gingerly next to the damaged package. He unfolded the newspaper piece by piece, reeling in the audience like a giant, singular fish gasping for air.

"You can . . . *transform*," he whispered, and the wad of crumpled newsprint he held in his palm quivered, producing a sensuous white dove. It then flew, circling the wildly applauding crowd once, twice, thrice, before perching on Nick's shoulder.

"*Leaves of Grass?*" I mouthed when we took our bows.

Nick beamed. "Brilliant, is it not?" he shouted above the applause. We bowed to the other side of the dingy theater. "Far better than the brick we used to use. A brick—what kind of message were we sending, anyway? Why, we might as well have shouted, 'Use violence, you brute!' No, indeed. But a book! The power of knowledge! To the masses!"

Nick thrust a fist in the air and practically floated offstage. I shook my head after him, but I couldn't help but grin. Leave it to Nick to worry about educating the masses in a crummy vaudeville theater. And he truly believed it could be done, city by city. Nick was out to alter the cosmos.

My father was a river rock, worn soft and smooth by years of tumbling water. Not like me, a rock that had been chipped and chiseled into something other than its original form.

Yes, Nick was flowery and flighty and, I believed, fragile. And yet here we were, in the midst of a band of con artists traipsing about the country.

Good thing he had me.

May 2, 1910

SIXTEEN DAYS

till the End of the World.

NEWS HEADLINE

Entire World Eagerly Awaits Comet

The dining car swayed as the train chuffed around a bend, and the gas chandeliers overhead flickered and tinkled. I gripped the back of one of the Cherry Sisters' chairs and shuffled sidewise to avoid toppling. Matilda Cherry smirked at me as if I'd just stolen one of her awful jokes, rather than simply righting myself. Blasted railways! If I ever break free from this vaudeville circuit, I'm never stepping foot in another railcar again.

I was late to dinner, and so would be dining alone. As per usual. My lack of friends my age didn't really bother me, except at mealtime. There were only four people younger than twenty on our circuit—well, five, now that Buster Keaton was here—and none of them spoke English. On longer jumps, when we'd been on the train for days, I'd tried striking up a conversation with the Frolov kids, who spoke Russian. It was exhausting, conversing with points and hand gestures and stick-figure drawings. They were nice, but still.

I drooped into a chair with my back to Mr. Whitting's, our road manager. I pushed my wrinkly green beans and gray meatloaf around on the plate.

I'm not sayin' the food in those dining cars
was bad, but I prayed after _I ate!_

Whitting's typewriter secretary sat opposite him, and it sounded as if she was taking notes as he talked around a mouthful of pasty mashed potatoes. I pitied her.

"No. Unh-unh," he mumbled. "Don't pay that fella one red cent until we figure out if it really was one of ours what painted his barn."

The secretary clicked the tip of her pen against the pad of paper. "Sure. Right. It was probably one of his _neighbors_ that scrawled 'The Greatest Show on Earth' with a big arrow pointing to the breeding stall."

I almost choked on a lump of bread.

"What's next, Nance?" Mr. Whitting mumbled. From the corner of my eye, I saw him lift his left hand. I knew from the way his chair nudged mine that he was smoothing long strands of hair across his bald head.

"Housekeeping," she said. "Going into Chicago, you know. Time to clean the bill."

Clean the bill? They were talking about who would be fired!

My ears perked up, and if I could've turned them front-side-back, I would've.

"Yep," Whitting said. "The blue envelopes. Yep. I rather enjoy trimming the fat from our troupe each year." Whitting was apparently also trimming the fat from his steak, the way his seat jimmied to and fro as he sawed at his dinner.

There must've been a lot of good left in Joe Whitting. Because none ever came out!

Whitting shoveled in another mouthful and said something else, something like, "Who do you think?" or "You really stink," or "My skivvies are pink." Probably was that first one, in hindsight.

Nancy, the secretary, apparently had problems understanding him, too. "Who do I think?" I felt Mr. Whitting's whole body shake with his nod.

"Hmmm . . . well, that trick cyclist is looking a little worse for wear," she said. "Frolov, right? But his kids are really good. Have you seen that one kid balance on one wheel while his brother does a handstand on his shoulders? You can't fire them."

Whitting grunted in agreement. Either that, or he just liked to grunt. And those who happened to know Joe Whitting knew that wasn't entirely out of the realm of possibility.

"Maybe that woman, you know, the one with the crazy peepers?"

Cross-Eyed Jane? I set my fork down and listened with every part of my body.

Whitting paused, and I hoped it was to swallow. "Yeah, she's tired," he said. "But that hag can peddle medicine like nobody I've ever seen. She still makes heaps of money for this outfit."

Nancy's pen went *tap-tap-tap* on her notepad. I thought I might be vibrating with a soft hum, I was eavesdropping so hard. And I don't know how else to explain it, but I somehow *felt* what was coming next.

"Maybe that magician?" she said. "You know, the one with his daughter?"

Erm . . . *pardon? I'm right here!*

"He's good, good tricks, but he always *talks* to the audience," Nancy said.

Whitting snorted and nodded.

"Right?" she said. "Who does he think he is, lecturing everyone like that? Is he trying to *teach* people or something? Just use the piano player like all the other performers, for heaven's sake!"

Whitting spat a burst of laughter and pounded the table with his fist. The silverware jangled.

"Maybe. Maybe," he said. "Let me think about it. I'll let you know who's going to be on this train when it pulls out of Chicago on the twentieth. And who won't."

Before I remembered where I was—in the dining car, which is essentially a garbage can on wheels—I inhaled in a low, slow breath. I shuddered past the stink to find a mixture of joy and panic at this latest development.

A way out! We might truly break free from this horrible small-small-time vaudeville circuit once and for all. Live in one city, one house.

But jobless meant, of course, no money. I'd have to start saving more money, today. Because there was no way we'd be without money. No way.

I wandered toward the passenger car, trailing my fingers along the velvet wallpaper lining the narrow, dim corridor.

One city. A home. With a garden and a kitchen and a bath that only Nick and I use—not an entire troupe.

Home. It's the only place you can scratch wherever it itches!

I knew I should tell Nick that our jobs were in danger. I knew I should tell him to stop shooting the bull with his audience and just use popular ragtime music, like all the other performers. But if I didn't tell him, maybe we'd be left behind—in *Chicago!*

I suppose I'm stating the obvious when I say that I hated vaudeville more than a bull hates his teasing matador. But Nick? His love of vaudeville was practically tangible, it was so intense. He loved everything about it: performing, his fellow performers, the props, the costumes, the audience—especially the audience. "Fresh minds," he'd call them. "Empty vessels, waiting to be filled."

If I am to be honest, I must admit that I'd fantasized about Nick getting fired before. But if a performer got fired in, say, Missoula, Montana, in Missoula he stayed. No "thanks for your years of hard work, Jack." Not even a "we'll give you a lift into civilization." Nope, when you got handed your hat, that was that. So the thought never appealed.

Until now.

We were barreling toward Chicago. Chicago—my hometown. We'd left it five long years ago. We'd returned every year on the circuit, and every year it felt as if my heart were ripped out through my fingertips when we chugged out of the LaSalle Street Station.

The door to the passenger car rolled open with a *clack-clack,* and the stench of cigar and pipe smoke billowed out. The aisle was so narrow, I had to walk sidewise between the maroon velvet seats. The chairs were grouped in fours—two facing the front of the train, two facing the rear—and each grouping had a small table that folded up from beneath the window, should the urge to do a little gambling strike. Which it oft did, to members of our troupe. Many of them played noisy games involving dice and cards, much to the chagrin of the other passengers trying to sleep in their seats.

I squinted through the reeking smoky fog and found Nick thumbing through a worn copy of *Civil Disobedience.* Disobedience, eh? Perhaps old Henry David Thoreau and I could teach each other a few tricks.

"Hope!" Nick placed a strip of yellow fabric between the pages of his book and folded it shut. He gestured to the seat opposite him and smiled such a warm smile, my cold thoughts about his getting fired melted a bit, and I was afraid they might pour right out of my mouth and puddle on the floor between us. I dropped into the crushed-velvet chair and tucked my legs beneath me.

"Hope, I was just telling Chekhov here"—at this, he waggled his fingers to the hairy gentleman sleeping next to him—"about Walt Whitman's theory of symbiosis, and how two organisms living and working together are far stronger than one. Care to add anything to our discussion, oh assistant of mine?"

At that, the gentleman, whom I thought had been sleeping, lifted one eyelid. Ever so imperceptibly, he shook his head at me. I knew how the fellow felt; I had been subjected to many an hour's discussion of old man Whitman. I'd had just over three years of formal schooling, but Nick often assigned me reading, or as he called it, "brain fertilizer." Which sounded an awful lot like "mind manure," which made Nick chuckle every time I said it.

"No thanks, Nick. Just came to say good night."

"Ah, retiring for the evening, are we? Let me leave you with a closing thought, then, compliments of Mr. Thoreau." He bent forward and retrieved from under his seat another book by Thoreau, this one titled *Walden*. Nick flipped open the soft leather book in his hands and began reading: "'Wherever I sat, there I might live, and the landscape radiated from me accordingly. What is a house but a *sedes*, a seat?'" I find that fascinating!" Nick beamed, slamming the book shut. "Wherever you are—*that's* your home! For the moment, at least. For isn't your own self your home? . . ."

Honestly. How do parents *do* that? It was as if Nick had been reading my mind.

He continued to ramble, but I stood. "Good night, Nick." I leaned over him and kissed him on the cheek. He somehow managed to smell of shaving soap underneath all that smoggy smoke.

He patted me on the back while still clutching *Walden,* and the pages rustled. "Sleep tight, Hopeful. For tomorrow— *Chicago!*"

A whoop went up from the table across the aisle. The new kid, Buster Keaton, raked a pile of chips toward his chest with his left arm. His face was stony, the perfect poker face, but from where I stood, I could see his right hand rubbing the outer seam of his trousers beneath the table. The trousers appeared to have quite a bit of wear and tear there. A nervous habit. The other gamblers at the table chortled and derided the loser, Winsor McKay, for being duped by a kid.

Nick bent back over his book, and I sidled up the aisle, his words ringing in my ears. *"Tomorrow—Chicago!"*

Yes. Tomorrow and forever.

Did you ever hear the one about the girl who does nothing to prevent her father from getting fired? No? Then stay in your seat, folks. This punch line has yet to be written.

I shimmied sideways through the narrow Pullman Palace Sleeping Car, which was draped in shades of Pullman green. Sometimes I believed if I saw one more yard of Pullman green fabric, I might vomit Pullman green. When I wasn't sleeping in a railcar, I bunked in a dingy room in a boardinghouse, usually with Cross-Eyed Jane as a roommate. I was fond of the old gal, sure, but seeing her in her skivvies tested the limits of our friendship.

Nick slept in the passenger car, right in his seat, like most of the performers. But he insisted on buying me a sleeper unit, saying it'd be improper for a young lady to sleep in her seat. I would've been grateful, except I knew how much money we could've saved if I had just snoozed alongside the rest of the troupe.

I reached my unit, folded back the velvety curtain, and pulled the cot down from the ceiling. I hoisted myself onto the bed and closed the curtain behind me, creating a nest of sorts. I then lifted my skirts and removed the *Chicago Daily Tribune* newspaper I'd stolen off the face of a snoring passenger in the smoke chamber I'd just left. The front-page headline read,

IS OUR WORLD TO BE DESTROYED BY COMETS?

My heart jumped, remembering the dark fear in the eyes of my crazed Coin yesterday. I skimmed the article, and it, like all the other articles I'd read, waylaid any fears. The story explained that while the Earth would indeed travel through the tail of Halley's Comet sometime between 11:20 p.m., May 18, and 1:20 a.m., May 19, no harm would befall its inhabitants.

I trusted science. I trusted anything that could be proven with logic and reason.

So why would anyone worry? Well, five years of performing magic on the vaudeville circuit taught me that people will believe what they want to believe. It also taught me that people at the top don't always know what they're talking about. I supposed that might include politicians and scientists, too.

I turned to the back portion of the newspaper, to the classified advertisements. I scanned the tiny print for the "For Let" section. But my eyes were first drawn to a different advertisement:

* * * * * * * * * * *

You can see Halley's Comet clearly with the naked eye if your eyesight is perfect. If, however, the comet is not clear and distinct, wear HARRIS GLASSES. They enable you to see just as nature intended.

And just below that:

* * * * * * * * * * *

Halley's Comet, like other comets, is a thing of mystery. But there is no mystery about our SAFE DEPOSIT BOXES. It is a cold, hard fact that they are absolutely fireproof.

Finally, I found what I was searching for:

* * * * * * * * * * *

TO LET TO REFINED PEOPLE. Furnished rooms, single or en suite. $2-$3/week. 3417 Prairie. Phone: Douglas 408.

I doubted that Nick and I would qualify as "refined," but I got what I needed from the ad. Nick and I would need two to three dollars a week for rent. An awful lot of money, considering I made about two cents every time I read tarot cards, after Jane and Whitting took their cuts.

Three dollars! Huck.

A spark of fear shot through me like a firecracker. I gazed

out the tiny compartment window, blackened by years of coal smoke billowing past it from the train engine. There was one small, clean portion through which I could see the outside world whizzing past, the world en route to Chicago. My hometown. I'd wager that none of my friends there would even recognize me. Most of my former friends would be finished with school, working steady jobs and living quiet lives. Lives without drama or stage lights or railcars or dead poets.

Outside the tiny window, rows of corn ticked by. Corn, corn, and more corn. From the ground, solid and true. I wanted my feet planted in the soil as firmly as that corn. If I were to have that by May 20, I needed to make a pile of money. Fast.

Above the ever-so-practical stalks of corn stretched the fantastically impractical skies. There were no clouds, and tonight the universe offered a dazzling light show. Stars and planets and, there! A tiny speck of light, just larger and brighter than a star, that was supposedly a comet barreling toward Earth.

Me, possibly being free from vaudeville in eighteen days.

A comet, possibly killing us all in sixteen.

The irony and apprehension and sheer ridiculousness of it all made my head light. I could already feel the effect of Halley's Comet, that great ball of ice teasing me with her million-mile tail of fizz.

May 3, 1910

FIFTEEN DAYS

till the End of the World.

NEWS HEADLINE

*The Flaming Comet: Few of Us Have Seen It, but All Are
Interested, and Many Seem to Be Worrying About It*

I could smell it before I could see it—Chicago! I closed my eyes
and inhaled deeply. The metallic stench of the meatpacking
plants battled against the syrupy smell of the confectioner fac-
tories. Coal smoke, budding trees, and a whiff of fishy Lake
Michigan.

Home.

Our train screeched to a lazy halt at the LaSalle Street Railroad Station, a chunky building that loomed thirteen stories
tall. It was four a.m., and already the city was bustling with activity. Streetlamps flickered showy flames, as if they knew
their light would soon become dwarfed by the sunrise. Massive
boats chugged toward the Rush Street Bridge, which, instead of
genuflecting with respect, pivoted gracefully en pointe, rotating

lengthwise so that it temporarily ran parallel to the Chicago River, rather than crossing it. Oxcarts burdened with hay puttered about. Carriages and noisy, motor-laden horseless carriages shared the same roadways, much to the horses' dismay.

My heart tugged as I stood on the corner of LaSalle and Van Buren, as it did every May when we returned to the city. A whole month in Chicago. It was the longest we'd stayed in any one locale in the five years I'd been traveling with the troupe. And it was *Chicago.*

I wouldn't say I'd been homesick for all these months. Home terminally ill was more like it.

The stagehands were unloading our props and costumes and tents from the railcars and stacking them onto carriages. The first day in a new city was always like this, eaten away by the logistics of moving one hundred people from town to town. Mr. Whitting calculated all those lost wages with each passing minute, and his puffy red face grew puffier and redder throughout the day. He began yelling the moment he stepped off the train. "Easy with that crate! You wanna be the one responsible for killing Happy the Monkey? Yo! Easy! That's fifty bucks worth of rope, mister!"

The performers lingered just long enough to watch their belongings make it safely from the train car to the carriage before tipping the stagehands and bolting off into the city like inmates on parole. Nick and I always took part in this custom, onlooking with great interest, though Nick had never figured out the importance of our doing this. He smiled and chatted with his fellow performers, not once realizing our purpose for overseeing the unload at every stop.

"Damn fella and his books!" Two stagehands hefted Nick's Herkert & Meisel trunk out of one of the storage cars and slammed it onto the ground. "They's no way this is under the weight limit!" The burlier one pointed at Mr. Whitting. "He's definitely haulin' more than just his props. You tell that guy to lighten his load, or I'll dump a gallon of paint on them books, I will!"

Nick laughed heartily, like it was all part of one big, ongoing gag he had with these guys. "Thanks for the muscle, fellas. Your good works will come back to you threefold." He lifted and tilted a tin of Sen-Sen breath mints toward them in a mock toast, then popped a handful of mints into his mouth. He returned to his heated discussion of state's rights with Bert Savoy, the troupe's female impersonator, who carefully picked his teeth with a long, red-polished pinky fingernail, so as not to muss his perfect red lipstick.

Why anyone would get in a debate with Nick is beyond me. He'd demand the last word with an echo!

Sure enough, the burly stagehand took a black-ink marker from his pocket and slashed a thick circle with a line through it across Nick's trunk. I sighed and strolled up to the stagehand.

"How much?"

He turned, then looked surprised when he had to drop his eyes to see who'd asked the question. He lifted one eyebrow at me. "What's that, girlie?"

"How much for you to cover that mark?"

He smiled at me with tobacco-stained teeth. "What mark?"

I thumped the black circle on Nick's trunk with my knuckles. "That mark. A quarter do?"

"Fifty cents."

"What? No way. Thirty cents."

The stagehand guffawed, his greasy hair falling in greasy clumps over his shoulder. "Forty-five."

No way could I spare forty-five whole cents on the cusp of Nick getting canned. I sighed and reached for my grouch bag. "Forty, and you guarantee that he doesn't get the treatment."

"Treatment?" The stagehand widened his eyes like an angel, pretending he had no idea what I was talking about.

I looked back at Nick, who was still chattering to an obviously bored Madame Bert. "C'mon, the treatment. You know . . ." I bulked up my shoulders and lowered my voice, doing my best imitation of a stagehand. " 'Aw, lookit that,' " I said in a growl, gesturing toward Nick's trunk. " 'All your magic props got broke into little tiny pieces.' " I dropped my shoulders and the imitation. "*That* treatment."

The stagehand nodded and held out his open palm. I dropped in four dimes. "And I wanna watch you cover that mark."

The muscle crammed the forty cents in his pants pocket,

took a huge white sticker from his breast pocket, licked it, and smacked it over the stain. WELCOME TO THE WINDY CITY! it read.

"Pleasure doing business with ya." The stagehand pointed at me and did this thing with his tongue, making a sound like *chick-chick.*

I nodded once and leaned in close for a sharp whisper. "And not a thing broken or I'll tell Mr. Whitting you guys are starting a union. Understood?"

The hand's Adam's apple bobbed and he blinked twice. "Got it."

I pointed back at him and made the same *chick-chick* sound. "Pleasure's been all mine." Especially since that would be the *last* time I'd ever have to tip a stagehand.

I became intimately familiar with the dark, narrow stairwell of the boardinghouse that would be our home base for the next three weeks. I'd climbed two flights of stairs once, helping Nick haul his overloaded trunk to the male floor. Then I'd climbed three flights twice, once helping Cross-Eyed Jane with her trunk, and once hauling my own trunk, solo. *Thump, thump, thump* all the way to the top, to the female floor.

I tugged my trunk across the threshold of my room. The walls boasted a mishmash of peeling wallpaper, which likely held the crumbling house erect. The wooden floors could be crossed in four longish paces, and the room held two stripped-bare mattresses, a bureau, and—oooh, high class!—a wash-basin.

*This room was so small, when you put the key
in the door, you broke the window!*

Except there *was* no window. Huck. I drooped onto the bed, which groaned, and kicked off my boots.

Cross-Eyed Jane was expertly pinning a turban about her head. How did she do that without a mirror?

Jane jutted her chin at my bare feet. "She should watch it," she said around the pins in her mouth. My toes dangled dangerously near a shallow dish of clear liquid, within which the legs of the bed stood. Within which a dozen or so ants floated, dead.

"Wha—what is that?" I asked, scrambling to tuck my feet up under me.

Jane removed the last pin from betwixt her lips. "Oxalic acid. Keeps the ants from reaching her while she sleeps."

*I'm not saying the house was dirty, but they'd
need a cleaning crew to visit before they could
demolish it.*

"She's coming to read cards later, lovey?" Jane asked.

I nodded. "Be down after Nick checks in. And, hey, Jane?"

"Hmmm?" Jane fastened necklace after necklace about her shoulders.

"You think there's any way we could charge more than a nickel?"

Jane paused to look me over. Erm . . . look *over* me. "Doubtful, love. Hope-girl charges a dime; she loses a lot of customers.

30

Coins, she calls her customers." Jane chuckled and resumed stacking on the jewels.

I nodded, but I thought Jane might be wrong on this one. Surely the Coins in Chicago could afford a dime. More people here, after all. And we definitely wouldn't lose over half our Coins, now, would we? That'd be the point at which we'd actually *lose* money. I was about to say all this when Nick walked in.

Did I mention? Nick didn't know about me and the Mademoiselle Ari bit. At least, I don't think he did. I decided when I started reading cards that it'd be easier not to tell him what I was up to. And he either never noticed or decided not to ask. Nick didn't exactly monitor me. He preferred instead that we be equals.

"Man on the floor! Man on the floor!" Nick said, peeking between slits in the fingers that covered his eyes. "Everyone decent?"

Honestly. Why must parents do such things?

Jane giggled and punched Nick on the arm. "Decent! Ain't a decent soul in vaudeville, and he knows it!"

Nick laughed. "Jane, I wouldn't be here if I believed that."

It was true. He wouldn't.

Jane winked at me—*near* me—and left the room, jingling and jangling.

Nick sat next to me on the bed. I pointed to the floor.

"Watch the acid," I said.

"I saw that," Nick said, nodding. "Poor ants never stood a chance."

"Poor ants," I said.

Nick smiled. "You excited to be back in Chicago?"

More than you could possibly know. I nodded and waited, hopeful. We'd just entered our hometown for almost three weeks—now was surely when we'd finally discuss my mother. Her illness. Her death. I wanted so badly for him to speak of her, I almost shouted out her name.

But instead Nick hugged me sidewise, with one arm about my shoulder. "Just don't get so upset when we leave this time, okay, Hopeful? Breaks my heart."

I knew he was trying to be nice, trying to soften the blow, but instead, his words sparked my anger. Didn't he *ever* wonder *why* I got so upset? Would he *never* speak of her again?

"You know," Nick said, oblivious to the questions pounding about in my head. "I've been thinking. I should talk to the audience a little more in our act, don't you agree? I think they quite enjoy our little chats."

This was, of course, exactly the opposite of what he should do, according to Whitting's secretary. I swallowed past the lump that dammed the words in my throat. *I should tell him now,* I thought. *Just say, "No, Nick, you shouldn't do that. You'll be fired from the job you love."*

But I didn't. I said nothing.

Nick patted my knee with a single, decisive pat. "Well, then, it's settled. We must give the crowd what they need, right, Hopeful?"

Right. I looked at the floor, at the legs of the bed and the dead ants floating about in a pool of acid. Poor ants never stood a chance.

"Want to go down to the beach?" Nick asked, rising and dusting the seat of his pants. Even he was leery of this sleazy boardinghouse.

"The beach" was not the shore of Lake Michigan, as most would assume. No, to vaudevillians, "the beach" was the stretch of land between the theater in which we'd perform and our boardinghouse. The beach was where all the performers lingered in their downtime, as the thought of returning to a scum hole like this house did not appeal. The beach was where the makeshift storefronts would be erected, where I would soon read tarot cards for money.

The last thing I wanted to do right now was go to the beach with Nick. No, I wanted to find my tarot-reading getup and start slapping down some cards, now that we were well on our way to getting fired.

But I couldn't do it, not after I kept silent about our jobs being in danger. "Sure," I said, and pulled on my boots. I hopped off the bed, and my heel nicked the edge of the bowl that held the oxalic acid. The liquid sloshed out of the dish, and two ants were swept onto the floor with it.

"Mind the ants!" Nick chirped and walked down the hallway.

Mind the ants. Right.

It was a sunny Chicago day, but like many here, the brisk wind carried a chill.

> *Chicago is so windy, a chicken here once laid*
> *the same egg six times!*

The wind caused me to hunch into my overcoat, making me feel small. I felt small, anyway, standing next to Nick on the

33

sidewalk. He was big, broad-shouldered, and blond. I was not. I was tiny for my age, with crazy-curly black hair to my waist and darkish skin. Even the hairs on my arms were dark. My smattering of moles and deep brown eyes told the tale of my absent parent.

Yes, Nick loomed next to me, as he always did. And yet today I felt particularly small. And dark.

"Lookit that," Nick said, lifting his chin toward the dozen or so tents that had already been erected on the beach. He shook six or seven Sen-Sen mints into his mouth from a tin that read, "Breath Perfume." Nick ate mints like most people ate peanuts—crunch and swallow. Very little enjoyment, for what it was worth.

"Already they're turning a quick buck." He shaded his eyes from the glaring sunlight to peer at the tents that papped in the wind.

Yes, they were. My fellow performers were turning a buck. My skin itched, I wanted so badly to be out there, turning a buck, too. I had but seventeen days until that train left without us on it.

We strolled alongside the tents, under which our fellow performers hawked handmade jewelry, knitted scarves, knives. Quite the assortment of junk. I knew most of it would break/unravel/disintegrate on May 21, the day after our train left.

Cross-Eyed Jane sat next to a scrolly sign that read, THE CROOKED EYE SEES ALL. PALMS READ, 5 CENTS. I snorted a laugh. That sign got me every time.

Medicines in tiny brown bottles fanned out from Jane like mighty fingers beckoning. She pinched a vial between her forefinger and thumb and shook it at the couple of Coins she'd snagged. "What do Indian Root pills do?" she was saying to them. "What *don't* they do? You gots rheumatism? Burns? Bruises? Sprains?" She leaned in closer and whispered, "The *piles*? This here'll cure it, and then some."

Nick clicked his tongue and shook his head. We walked a few more steps. I wanted to ask him the difference between peddling medicines and peddling magic, but I held my tongue.

The next tent saw quite a lot more action. Half a dozen pluggers paced about the tent anxiously, waving the wads of sheet music they were selling above their heads. They sang, they hollered, they cajoled—they did everything they could to gather a crowd about them. And it was working. Nick and I stood at the edge of the crowd and looked on.

"Step right up, folks! Sheet music! Sheet music, five cents!"

"We got your 'Halley's Comet Rag' music here, folks. We got 'The Comet and the Earth.' "

"The latest and greatest vaudeville music is all here, folks, five cents!"

"The comet! The comet! The comet I've seeeeeeen! I wonder how bright it will beeeeeeeam!"

A crowd of twenty-some-odd townies had gathered before this tent. One of the pluggers thrust forward the sheet music for "A Trip to the Moon." The cover featured a propeller-driven hot-air balloon toting high-society patrons toward the moon, while a comet plowed toward Earth.

A local wearing a particularly distasteful expression swatted the sheet music aside. "You take the threat of Halley's Comet so lightly!" he growled.

The plugger looked over his shoulder at his fellow salesmen and shrugged. They all shared a laugh and resumed their peddling.

"Sheet music, folks! One jitney!"

" 'The Comet March and Two-Step' right here!"

"You laugh!" yelled a member of the crowd of patrons. "But the Earth will soon pass through the tail of the terrible comet! Poisonous gasses will fill the heavens!"

"Get your souls saved now!" someone else from the crowd yelled.

"Close your windows and keep indoors!"

The crowd grumbled like a pack of wolves, and my heart thumped in my ears as I watched their fear grow. Isn't it odd how fear feeds on fear? Nick, in one of his rare bouts of acting like a parent, encircled my waist with his arm and steered me back to Cross-Eyed Jane's tent. She was still hawking her cure-alls.

I peered over my shoulder at the faces of the crowd members behind me, now warped with twisted, red anger. The pluggers laughed at them hardily.

"Nick?" I asked.

"Hmm?"

"Are you worried about this comet?"

Nick pulled the tin of mints from his pocket and offered me some. I shook my head, and he tipped the tin up to his mouth. "No," he said finally around the mints in his mouth. "But unfortunately, there are some superstitious imaginations that cannot look upon anything unusual without fear."

Nick turned and studied the crowd, rubbing his jaw and nodding, as if they were comprised of something he was not.

"Their minds are rather close to the animal mind, are they not? They are akin to the horse that shies time and time again at a scrap of paper."

The Sen-Sen mints cracked between his teeth. "Poor, simple souls. What those folks need is hope."

At that moment, it was almost as if the tail of the comet reached out and tapped me singly, sparking a most electric thought. I looked from the angry crowd of locals to the care-not pluggers to Cross-Eyed Jane and her medicines to Nick.

Money. Medicine. Mints.

Yes, those people needed hope.

And I was just the one to sell it to them. In pill form.

And thus, Hope's Anti-Comet Pills were born.

May 4, 1910

FOURTEEN DAYS
till the End of the World.

NEWS HEADLINE

Approaching Plunge of the Earth Through
the Tail of Halley's Comet

The troupe gathered backstage at the Orpheum Palace Theatre, the theater where we'd perform over the next fifteen days. First, allow me to address the misnomer *palace*: This drafty old firetrap was anything but. There were no toilets, no sinks—no running water whatsoever. The filthy walls bore cracks that looked like scars, tears in the plaster that cut so deep, it looked as though the wind and rain could jump right through. The floors were broken and uneven, so much so that Bert Savoy had to lift up his skirts to walk, lest his hemline get snagged on a snarly nail. The theater was small for a city the size of Chicago, its smattering of benches holding only a hundred-some-odd occupants.

*One nice thing about those small theaters: You
had no room for complaints!*

Whitting must've noticed the sour faces on his performers. "No moaning about this place. Whattaya want? It's got an orchestra pit!" he said, presumably to keep his performers happy. Or off his back.

"No three-piece band here!" he said. The troupe chuckled and nodded.

A three-piece band in vaudeville: a piano, a piano player, and a stool. The usual musical accompaniment in the sticks.

Did I mention? Nick and I toured the small-small-time vaudeville circuit. We were rookies, with a mere five years in. Acts on this circuit were either new, like us, or on their way out of show business completely. Our circuit was so small-time, the managers referred to us as the peanut circuit. The performers called it the death trail. The performers were far more accurate.

Just about all of vaudeville—the small-small-time, the small-time, and the big-time circuits—were owned by one gentleman: Mr. Benjamin Franklin Keith. I'd never met him. I never hoped to, from what I'd heard.

*I've heard B. F. Keith had no enemies.
But his friends didn't like him.*

"Okay, folks, gather round." Mr. Whitting stood on a dilapidated wooden chair and clapped. He nearly toppled and righted himself by palming the head of one of the Frolov kids. Aleksandr, I believe.

"Okay, everyone, the oath is in your mailbox. Get it, sign it right now, and pass it forward."

The performers straggled over to a line of dusty cubbyholes, found their mailboxes, and retrieved the slips of paper therein.

Nick plunked the sheet of paper onto the table and uncapped his pen. He was just touching pen to paper when I caught his hand.

"Just a second," I whispered. I'd learned to reread the oath in each new city, just in case Whitting or any other manager decided to slip in some new rules on us. The oath read,

Don't say "slob" or "son of a gun" or "hully gee" onstage unless you want to be canceled peremptorily. If you do not have the ability to entertain Mr. Benjamin Franklin Keith's audience without risk of offending them, do the best you can. Lack of talent will be less open to censure than would be an insult to a patron. If you are in doubt as to the character of your act, consult Mr. Whitting before you go onstage, for if you are guilty of uttering anything sacrilegious or even suggestive, you will be immediately closed and will never again be allowed in a theater where Mr. Keith is an authority. I hereby pledge to abide: _____

Nope, no new rules. Just the usual threats. "Okay, sign," I said, sliding the piece of paper back across the table to Nick.

The troupe passed their signed oaths forward, and Whitting

counted them before proceeding. "All right, good, good. Next on our agenda: stealing."

A grumble arose from the performers. Things always turned up missing on our circuit. Performers knew better than to leave precious items like silver-plated hairbrushes or silk suspenders lying about.

Whitting picked at a blob of tobacco in his teeth. "Rumor on the circuit is that this latest boardinghouse is a real black hole, ha ha. As in, things you bring in sometimes don't make it out. Hide your stash. And as always, the Keith Circuit is in no way responsible for items that disappear."

The performers shifted and murmured. This warning was nothing new. Seemed every boardinghouse manager across the United States had sticky fingers. The troupe wanted to get to the real business: the call-board.

"All right, here we go, folks, the new call-board." Whitting thumped a piece of cardboard standing on an easel. It was covered with a ratty sheet. "But before I unveil it, I wanna say: I don't want to hear a single one of you piss and moan about your spot on the bill, got it?" He pointed a chewed-on stumpy cigar at the troupe. "I hear any complaints, and the lot of you will be looking for work."

Ah, Joe Whitting. His friends could be counted on the missing arm of a one-armed man.

"Here you go!" Whitting whisked the sheet off the call-board, and a cloud of dust made everyone hack and wheeze. Whitting stood next to the board, smiling and nodding and chewing on his cigar. It was apparent that he enjoyed the sense of power that came with shuffling us performers around on the bill.

The performers ignored Whitting's threats, as they often did, and immediately bemoaned their allotted slots.

"I have to follow the Cherry Sisters? All that rotten fruit thrown onto the stage? Disgusting!"

"Better than following the Chekhovs. That monkey of theirs craps all over the place!"

My eyes flew to our slot—there, number three on the bill, "Magician and his Assistant." I wondered each time I saw that if the managers even realized I was the magician's daughter.

Number three—hmmm. Not a bad slot. Respectable, but nothing too grand. It's no slot eleven, but then, no one in this troupe would hold the headliner spot so long as the Three Keatons were touring with us.

I turned to Nick, certain he'd be fine with the new bill. But his brow was furrowed and he was popping mints into his mouth.

"Three's good," I whispered.

"Yes, but look at our lead-in," he said. I looked at who was slotted at number two: Dr. Electricity. Nick abhors Dr. Electricity. Check that—Nick abhors all that Dr. Electricity represents. It'd be hard to hate the man himself—wimpy, snuffling Dr. Electricity does not lead the life of a flashy vaudevillian. Unless you count his hobbies. All things new and pulsing, like electric lightbulbs and kinetoscopes and wireless telegraphs, appealed to Dr. Electricity. And he demonstrated them all in his act.

"To follow an act of such blatant progressivism!" Nick rubbed his temples as if he had just witnessed a horrible crime and was trying to rid the image from his brain. "His gadgets—those awful, throbbing, noisy contraptions—the demise of society!"

Did I mention? Nick was prone to overreacting. But I knew just how to handle this one.

"You know," I said, twisting a lock of hair. "You follow him, Nick, and *you* get the upper hand. You get to counter any point he makes. He says science, you say nature. You get the final say."

Nick stopped rubbing his head and opened his eyes. "I think I see your strategy here, Hopeful." He popped three more mints in his mouth. "Yes, yes, indeed. Perhaps fate led us to this slot, eh? Perhaps we have been placed in a slot of divine countenance!"

Nick strode off whistling with renewed purpose before I had much of a chance to consider what he meant. I shrugged it off and searched the faces of the other performers before I found who I was looking for: Buster Keaton.

Buster stood among a group of three or four adults, nodding and chatting and smacking Hubert Williams on the back.

"Couldn't agree with you more!" Buster said. He talked to adults like he was one. He was tall for his age, true, but it was more than that. He seemed truly comfortable around the other older performers. "Can't stand the southern circuit, my-self."

I swallowed and adjusted the waist on my dress before approaching the group. What was I *doing*? I didn't know Buster.

What if he laughed at me? Worse, what if he turned me in to Whitting? And worse yet, what if he stole my idea? He was a headliner, after all; they could get away with just about anything. But my instincts told me this fellow could be trusted. And yet, he had to be a *little* cutthroat if he'd made it all these years in vaudeville. Trustworthy and cutthroat. My kind of guy.

Everyone made a huge to-do when Buster and his mom and dad joined our circuit. They were big-time performers. Big. Time. Rumor had it the only reason they were here was because they were being punished for something. Oh, huck. Could he be trusted?

I tucked my hair behind my ears and took a deep breath. *Stop it, Hope,* I told myself. *You're being ridiculous. He's just another person. And you need him to pull this thing off.*

I tapped him on the shoulder. I had to stand on tiptoe to do it. Buster eased around and slid his thumbs under his suspenders.

"What can I do you for, kid?" he asked.

I smirked. "Kid? You're not much older than I am."

The crowd of adults laughed and turned away. Buster's dark eyes were deep set, his nose and jawline sharp and narrow. Handsome, behind that face of stone he was famous for. We stood like that for one awkward moment too long.

He raised his eyebrows at me. "Yes?"

I filled my lungs with air as discreetly as possible. "I need to borrow your clothes."

"My clothes?"

Oh, huck. That came out wrong. "No, um, just one outfit, really."

Buster coolly looked me over from head to toe. "No way you can fit into my clothes."

It was true. He was a good two heads taller than I. But I knew that already. "That's okay," I said. "Actually for the best."

"What do you need them for?"

Here we go. I licked my lips. I'd decided it would be easier to tell the truth on this one, as the truth sounded more like a lie than a lie would. "I'm going to sell anti-comet pills and I want to be dressed as a boy to do it so people will trust me."

Buster didn't nod, didn't shake his head, didn't react in any detectable way. I had to hand it to him. The guy was perfectly aloof. Here was this tiny wisp of a girl asking him for a pair of his trousers so she could peddle anti-comet pills, and he hardly blinked an eye.

"No," he said at last. I thought my chest might implode, it tensed so rapidly. What did he mean, *no*? No trousers? No deal? Was he going to sell me out?

But then he began rubbing the outer edge of his trousers, like I'd seen him do in the poker game.

"No, you shouldn't dress like a boy. Comet pills—"

"*Anti*-comet pills," I corrected.

"*Anti*-comet pills," he continued, "would be more believable coming from a girl."

"Excuse me?"

"Folks wouldn't think a young girl is pulling a fast one on them, see? It's actually perfect. Young, fresh-faced thing, peddling medicines."

I might've turned eight shades of crimson on that one.

"No, dress like yourself, kid."

"Don't call me kid."

He shrugged, the most reaction I'd managed to elicit thus far. "What are you going to use as pills?"

I was surprised that he'd taken such an interest. I peered at him, but he seemed genuinely interested, and not in the sense of stealing-my-idea interested. I pulled a tin of Sen-Sen mints that I'd borrowed from Nick out of my petticoat.

Buster nodded at the tin, rubbing his hand over the back of his neck. "Now, see, *that's* going to need the disguise."

"I'm sorry?"

"Kid, you're going to have to doctor up those pills in some way. You think folks won't recognize that you're peddling Sen-Sen breath mints?"

Now it was my turn to shrug. I'd not considered that.

"And this tin," he said, flipping the lid lightly. "You're gonna need some new packaging, too. You want I should draw up something for you?"

I believe I felt myself nod dumbly. This guy was *good.*

"Okay, then, kid. I'll come up with something and we'll get this little hoax of yours underway."

I found my voice again. "Don't tell Whitting about this. I'm not interested in giving him a twenty-five percent cut. And *don't* call me kid."

I strode away, feeling both victorious and panicked. I had fourteen days. Two scant weeks to rake in as much money as I could until Halley's Comet paid her visit. And now, I apparently had a partner.

Our first show in Chicago. I was onstage, squinting against the glare of the stage lights, when a stagehand shoved a huge, sparkly box on wheels from backstage, and I stopped its squeaky progress with the palms of my hands.

I'd decided that maybe—*maybe*—it would be okay to nudge our act a little closer to the blue envelope that would get us fired. I'd decided to flub the trick. What I was doing was awful. I knew this. But having a home—that was an honorable quest, was it not? Yes, yes, of course it was.

I licked my lips. *Here we go.*

I shot Nick the look I'd practiced all morning. The look was a combination of mock surprise and real regret. The look I shot him said: *The Saw-in-Half box? We're doing Saw-in-Half today?*

Isn't it amazing how much harder it is to lie through your eyes than through your teeth?

Nick scanned me, and I knew at once he realized my "mistake": I was wearing the purple ballet flats of my levitation costume. Purple ballet flats are hard to miss. He'd have to pull out all the stops to cover up this one.

"My daughter, ladies and gentlemen—" He took the fingers of my right hand and lifted them over my head, coaxing me to spin like a ballerina for the audience. I knew then exactly how angry he was. He never introduced me. His doing so now was his way of saying, *the fault lies entirely with her.* Or so it seemed.

"Hope here keeps me on my toes," Nick said.

Then, a spark of showmanship flashed through Nick's eyes.

47

As I spun in tiny circles, he gestured with his free hand to my purple pointed toes. Gestured *directly* to those awful purple shoes. "And I on hers!"

The crowd laughed. And just like that, his anger dissipated.

Nick was nothing if not gutsy. Now everyone in the audience had been alerted to the fact that I was wearing obscenely purple ballet flats. He had, in essence, just made this trick that much more difficult to pull off. He loved a challenge, my father.

Nick clicked open the locks on the Saw-in-Half box. "Consider this," he was saying. He splayed the Saw-in-Half box and patted its interior. I climbed inside, lying down lengthwise. My neck, hands, and purple feet draped across awkward half-moon cutouts in the box. Curse this trick! It simply did not get more uncomfortable than the Saw-in-Half bit.

"One of our *previous performers* would lead you to believe that you must acquire *things*—geegaws and gimcracks and games—to make yourself happy." Nick was making an all-too-obvious reference to Dr. Electricity, who had just finished demonstrating an unbelievably amazing doodad called a phonograph. Nick eased the top of the crate shut over me and fastened the sturdy wrought-iron locks with a *click*! It was like a coffin, except my head, hands, and feet were trapped outside the box, dangling like the appendages of a rag doll. The muscles in my neck burned with the effort of keeping my head upright.

Blasted Saw-in-Half box! Perhaps I could take an axe to this abomination and chop it into firewood for use in our new home.

I shook my head to rid it of yet another traitorous thought.

"But I say we must *detach* ourselves from the lure of material goods!" Nick pounded his fists on the lid of the box.

Oh, huck. He's doing his detachment lecture.

"Detachment," Nick said, stressing the theme of his chat. He pulled a flint from his pocket and held it brazenly forth to the audience.

Detachment? The crowd murmured. *What does he mean by . . . ?*

Nick then whisked—from where? Thin air?—an imposing machete, which gleamed like a mirror under the white-hot spotlights. The guests choked on their own gasps: *detachment*!

Allow me to pause to underscore that reaction. Detachment . . . Saw-in-Half . . . I know—I groaned every time I heard it, too. Nick thought the correlation was genius. I thought it was a stretch of logic at best and gruesome at worst.

Nick dragged the flint across the blade with an aching *screee* five, then six times, sending shivers down the spines of our audience. He then placed the flint and the machete on a table, strolled to the end of the box where my purple feet protruded, and slowly began pulling the box in a wide circle.

"Let us consider for a moment our society's imminent need for detachment." Nick said, spinning, spinning, faster and faster. "We buy things, we love things, we *need* things. . . ." While Nick chatted and spun, I pulled my purple-clad feet inside the box and felt around the lower half of the box with my toes. I found the dummy feet that lay in wait and kicked them out through the holes. The dummy feet wore black patent leather shoes. As I should've been.

"And yet our lives, our beautiful, blessed lives, depend on so few things external. Food. Shelter. Clothing. Plain and simple."

Simple. Pah! Next, I curled my knees all the way up toward my chest, folding myself completely into the upper half of the box. I'm small and can do this, but it's far from simple.

One might think that such motions are obvious to our crowd of onlookers, but Nick rotates the box from the end where real feet are exchanged for fake feet, and thus blocks most of my shuffling from view. Plus, he babbles the entire time. It is most distracting.

"So we must slow the ever-maddening cycle of acquiring, acquiring, acquiring, and start to recognize things for what they are: *things*. Goods should not rule us. *Money* should not rule us!"

The spinning slowed and Nick, the box, and I came to a rest, but I still felt as though I was spinning out of control.

Nick picked up the machete and twisted it in his wrists, making beams of light shoot forth off its surface. My neck burned with strain, my legs tingled in their cramped quarters. I shuffled as best I could in that hot, horrible box. Nick took notice of my discomfort, and smiled down at me—his warm, genuine smile, not his gleaming large show-business smile. I was forgiven for the shoes. And then I felt worse than before.

Nick hefted the silvery machete aloft, grasping it in both hands. "Detach thyself from the tyranny of *stuff*!" The machete slammed down through the precut notch in the Saw-in-Half box. It took considerable skill, maneuvering that knife the way he did, for the machete was indeed real, and the slot in the box, narrow. Nick successfully drove the machete toward its destiny. It popped the latch on the undercarriage of the box, separating the crate into two halves. And as this blasted box was on wheels, the lower half of it careened in one direction, the top half, with my entire body therein entwined, another.

Picture this: me, curled up tight, trapped in a box, wheeling along, defenseless. A rather fitting depiction of my life, wouldn't you by now agree?

At last, I wheeled to a halt. I was perfectly intact, of course—cramped, but intact. But the audience shrieked as if my blood had spattered across their creamy faces.

As part of the finale, I'm supposed to turn my head and smile at the crowd, a small miracle considering both my posture and my patience. Instead I managed to nod and wriggle my wrists as a sign of my enduring life. Nick stood right next to the tell-tell shoes, even going so far as to lean over them in a deep bow to accept the applause from the audience.

Not one soul noticed those blasted black shoes.

Or so I thought.

Backstage, Buster leaned against a dirty wall, a Sears, Roebuck Catalogue tucked into the crook of his arm.

> *The fellow looked so smug, I pictured him walking down lover's lane holding his own hand.*

"Nice shoes," he said, lifting his chin at my purple ballet flats. I bit my lip and slid my eyes to Nick, but he was already drifting away, buoyed by successfully overcoming my mishap.

"What's that?" I asked, pointing to the book.

"Sears catalogue."

Right. "I can see that. What's it for?"

He flipped open the catalogue to a page he'd marked therein: pharmacopoeias. The page was jammed with colorful illustrations of bottles, tubes, and tins. Cod liver oil, Morse's Indian Root Pills, and Comstock's Dead Shot Worm Pellets. Each boasted "miraculous medicinal results" from "cure-alls developed under the most rigorous scientific analysis."

"And . . . ?" I said. What was it with this guy and awkward moments, anyway?

"What kind of packaging you want for your comet pills, kid?"

"*Anti*-comet pills," I said. I'd already given up on the "kid." I scanned the page and pointed to a bottle of Dickinson's Witch Hazel. The label was extraordinary—a decrepit old witch held a broom in one hand and a lit candle in the other. She crouched next to two scratchy witch hazel bushes, the very picture of mystery.

"You can draw something like that?" I asked.

"Child's play," he huffed.

Well, isn't that a pip. I crossed my arms and glared at him. "You had something else in mind?"

He flipped a page and pointed to an item: "The world-famous La Dore's Bust Food," the description read. "Unrivaled for its purity and guaranteed to create a plump, full, rounded bosom."

"Honestly!" I said. I turned the first two of eight shades of crimson, but then I saw what appeared to be a grin raising half of Buster's face. I couldn't help myself; I laughed.

"Draw whatever you want," I said with a smile.

"Whatever I want," he echoed, as though it had been a long time since anyone had considered what he wanted. He clapped the catalogue shut with one hand and turned to walk away.

"But start drawing it today, okay?" I said. "And Buster?" I yelled over the music onstage. The stagehands whipped toward me with a collective *"Shhhhh!"*

"Hmm?"

"Make it befitting of a pill that will save your soul."

That evening, while Cross-Eyed Jane was at the beach reading palms, I stole down to the kitchen and borrowed a jar of honey, a bag of flour, and two bowls. Back up in my nasty room, I took a single Sen-Sen breath mint and dipped it first into the bowl of honey, then rolled it in flour. It was a lumpy mess. And a no.

Back to the kitchen for jam. Jam+flour=even bigger mess. No.

Ditto with molasses, egg whites, and maple syrup. No, no, and no.

I popped a mint into my mouth, the bitter licorice taste making my mouth pucker. How could Nick stand these things? I sucked on the mint and looked at the mess I'd made. I had to clean this up before Jane returned.

I felt guilty about not giving Jane a cut, but I needed every bit of money I could make. And selling anti-comet pills would be much, much easier than reading crummy tarot cards, making a mere two cents per. It may be a little less honest, but . . . no, I needed the money. My father would be fired! I'd only sell comet pills—*anti*-comet pills—until I had enough money to support Nick and myself for a few weeks. Just a couple of days to pad my grouch bag, right?

So no, no cut for Jane. I was even hiding this scheme from the tour managers so I wouldn't have to give them a cut. That, if discovered, would almost certainly get Nick fired. Here it was, May 4—almost 5!—and I had thirteen short days before we traipsed through the comet's tail. No, I had to let as few people as possible know what I was up to with this hoax before Nick got fired.

The taste of the mint suddenly made me feel sick, and I spit it into a mound of flour.

It coated the sticky mint beautifully.

And thus was born my production process: mint+ water+flour=Anti-Comet Pill.

May 5, 1910

THIRTEEN DAYS

till the End of the World.

NEWS HEADLINE

To Escape the Comet, Hire Submarine Boat

Psst! Hope? *Hope!*"

I awoke to my name being whispered. As always, it took me a moment to remember where it was I had taken to sleep. In a dingy boardinghouse. In Chicago. And I had done so in my crinolines. Blast it!

"Hope!" Sleep left me slowly. I fought its departure.

> ***Mother Nature made one blunder: Mornings are too early!***

I blinked and tried to focus on the bed opposite mine. No Jane.

"Hope!" It came from the hallway. I shook off my sleep, crossed to the door, and opened it. "Buster?" I swung the door closed to a crack lest he get too close a look at my crumpled state. "What are you doing on the girl's floor? What time is it?"

"Six a.m., lazy bones. Get dressed. You've got customers."

"What?" I swung open the door, forgetting to be worried about my appearance.

"You're already dressed." He scanned me with a disapproving glance.

I smirked. "No peek at the skivvies today, chum."

He shrugged, and I couldn't tell if that had been his intention or not. "Got the pills ready?"

I ducked inside, grabbed the flour-coated goodies, and returned.

"They look good," he said, holding a pill up to the window. He turned to me. "Want to see the tin?"

His voice betrayed his excitement, because his face remained stony. I smiled to myself, knowing that Buster had been working on this project since the moment he'd left me backstage.

Buster held the tin before him as a peacock holds its tail. He'd glued a yellowing sheet of paper to the box. The tin now looked worn and dusty—nice touch. The lettering on the box scrolled and arched and announced glorious asylum from Mr. Halley's beast: Hope's Anti-Comet Pills, an Elixir for Escaping the Wrath of the Heavens. 25 cents each.

"A quarter?" My head shot up and I glared at Buster. "I can't charge a quarter for these! I only charged a nickel for my tarot readings, and that was outer limits!"

Buster jerked his head toward a crowd outside. I allowed myself a quick peek out the dingy window. There must've been twenty people! My every muscle seized.

"Every pocket out there is lined with a bunch of clinky quarters, just waiting for you."

I swallowed and nodded and looked at the tin again. "You put my name on it," I whispered, but Buster was too busy poking his finger against the dirty glass, counting the number of people gathered outside. It chilled me to think of those people out there—those Coins—knowing my name. That would not do. No, I'd have to cover that up with my thumb. No way would those people—*Coins*—know my name.

My eye was then drawn to the sketch: a blazing comet, barreling toward Earth, bearing the face and horns of Beelzebub himself. Below that, dozens of people with horrid expressions on their faces, scampering in an attempt to escape the wrath. Some were vomiting, some were clutching their throats while their eyeballs bulged in their sockets, some were even melting in their shoes. In the midst of all the chaos stood a calm, raven-haired young lady—me—wielding off the comet with a silvery shield, standing in a puddle of blood and guts. Positively gruesome.

My eyes widened. "That sketch—it's perfect."

He bounced on his toes. "I know. Let's go."

A motley crew had gathered outside the boardinghouse, most of them clutching hand-printed flyers. The papers they held, crumpled in their fists, announced the sale of a mystical potion that would allow those who partook to "survive and walk the ruins of the Earth." Buster had been busy!

I paused in the entryway and surveyed the Coins. The people in the crowd ranged in age from twenty to ninety, ranged in means from the wealthy to the penniless, ranged in temperament from the intense to the docile. But their *eyes* were all filled with fear.

I quickly lowered my gaze. *No eye contact,* I thought. *Nothing that would make me actually see these people. Erm...* Coins.

I licked my lips. *Here we go.* I swung open the front door.

"That's her!" A scruffy young fellow pointed at me. "She's the one!"

In seconds, the crowd buzzed about me like angry bees. Merciful heavens, did they reek! Huck! It was a good thing we were far enough down the beach that Cross-Eyed Jane and the other peddlers couldn't see what we were up to.

"You've got ze comet pills, dah?"

"How do they work? How many do I need?"

"I need at least a dozen—one for each of my family members."

They pawed at me and breathed stinking rotten breath in my face. One woman clawed at my dress and ripped the sleeve at the shoulder. "You can't hoard them!" she said, eyes flashing. "You must share!"

It was immediately apparent that selling anti-comet pills was going to be a lot more dangerous than reading tarot cards. And a lot more profitable. I took note that I was trembling. I needed to act fast, before I thought about this too much.

"Form two lines!" I cupped my hands around my mouth and yelled at the crowd. "Two lines, and everyone will get the pills they need."

Amazingly, the crowd obeyed. They parted into two rough

queues. As they organized themselves, they shared their theories:

"I hear they had to relight the furnace in the White House. Speculation is the comet is stealing the heat from the Earth."

"Za! 'Tis no speculation! A devil sit inside and drive it!"

"My cousin works for the gub'ment, and says folks'll be safe underwater. Rush of correspondence asking about them submarine boats, they've had."

"That fiery beast carries the influenza germ in her belly!"

I had been hesitant before, but that positively paralyzed me. *Influenza.* In the ear of my memory, I heard it: my mother's never-ceasing cough. It consumed me whole, and for the next few moments, I heard nothing but.

I cannot do this. I cannot.

Buster must've seen the pause in my eyes because he stepped forward and unfolded my grasp on the tin. "One quarter per pill, folks." He began exchanging mints for money. "Protect you and your loved ones now, before it's too late."

Three, then four transactions took place, and I was still looking on dumbly.

"At least one pill a day for best effects," Buster continued. "Come back tomorrow, ma'am. Tomorrow."

A scrappy old man approached us. He was hunched, and his face bore a striking resemblance to corkboard. "Is there a guarantee?"

A guarantee? I looked at Buster, and I actually saw that stone face of his twitch, almost imperceptibly, lifting the corner of his mouth. I knew he was thinking what I was thinking: If these pills *didn't* work, these folks would all be dead. Or so went the logic of one who would purchase anti-comet pills in the first place, right?

"If these pills don't work, the kid here will personally refund your money." Buster put his hand on my head like I was his loyal pup. And here I was beginning to grow fond of him.

And *refund*? Is he nutty? Of course, Nick and I will be in a whole different part of the city by the time refunds are demanded. Or, too, there's always the possibility that a deadly comet makes all refunds moot. I shuddered.

"Yes, siree," Buster said. "These pills are guaranteed to protect the purchaser from all cometary evils."

Sure enough, the scrappy old fellow bought one. I watched as Buster took his quarter and pocketed it.

That did it. I stood on tiptoe and pried the tin out of Buster's strong grip.

"You got it, folks!" I yelled to my crowd of Coins. But I made certain to avoid their eyes, to cover my name on the tin. "A pill or two under your belts each day will allow you to walk unscathed over the ruin of the world."

I wouldn't say my family was odd, but my wrists were now cuffed to a splintery piece of plywood while my father hurled knives at me.

To be honest, I didn't mind the knife-throwing bit. My only true discomfort in this trick was the itchy Victorian-era dress that Nick thought to be stylish for a girl my age. It had a high neck trimmed in ancient lace, which made my neck burn red. And the print! I'd seen walls bedecked in a similar print, I'm certain of it. Huge orange flowers, stacked one upon another, with yellow buds and green leaves fighting for air between them. Let's just say the gentlemen suitors didn't line up to fill my dance card when I wore that saucy little number.

But I was in rare spirits. I had sold out of pills earlier. The ten dollars and seventy-five cents I made weighed down my grouch bag, making the pockets of my dress sag, yet I couldn't remember the last time I felt so light.

Buster hadn't asked for a cut; in fact, he had willingly forked over the few quarters he'd pocketed when I was dazed. And I sure didn't offer him any money. No, the time would come when he'd ask for a cut, and I'd figure out what to do then. I'd likely have to sever our ties.

"The *point*," Nick said, lightly tapping the tip of an eight-inch knife with his finger, as if to demonstrate its ferocity. "The point is not that we can make ourselves happy with *things*." Nick then turned to face me, swept the knife in a graceful arc above his head, and whisked it at me. The audience gasped as the silvery knife flipped end over end through the air and lodged in the plywood mere inches from my skull.

Or rather, that's what they *thought* they saw. In actuality, Nick would slyly tuck the blades into a hidden pouch inside his overcoat. My job was to lightly press a button at the bottom of the board with my toe, which caused a knife handle to spring forth from the board to which I was anchored. Timing was everything in this bit. Done flawlessly, it most certainly appeared that Nick was casting knives at his only daughter.

Nick whisked the next knife from the holster about his waist.

"Because honestly," Nick bellowed, jabbing the knife toward

the crowd to underscore his theme, "we need so little. But we think we need so much! And why is that? Why, we might as well be strapped to a board while manufacturers and newspapers hurl their knives of advertisements at us again and again and *again*!"

As he grunted that last word, he rotated his arm and shoulder in an exaggerated throw, palmed the knife, and tucked it into his overcoat. I tapped the button with my toe, and the knife handle sprung forth from behind the board with a satisfying *whang*! The audience gasped. Nick winced, and I knew immediately that he'd injured himself. But he shrugged it off, and his brilliant smile barely flickered.

Nick was still quite crafty with his sleight-of-hand. Even I rarely caught him tucking away his knives on this bit. And the knives, while dull of blade, bore a nasty point. He'd punctured himself numerous times on the tips of those tricky things.

But when I saw the amount of blood dripping from his palm, I knew this was a serious injury. He retrieved the next knife from his holster and shivered when it touched his sensitive wound.

My pulse quickened as I watched his blood *drip-drip-drip* onto the stage. Yet Nick's lecture continued: "Their steely, sharp lies tell us we need, need, need! You know what we need? The spider spinning her web. The ebb and flow of the waves. The stars dancing in the vast night skies . . . ," he was saying, though I barely heard a word.

My one parent, I thought. *The only one left.* My mother died here, in this city. It couldn't be possible that I stood here, watching my father in pain?

Panic filled me as I thought of all the possibilities for that injury: It could get infected. Need stitches. Never clot. Bleed for days. Need to be amputated. And then where would we be?

Did you ever hear the one about the one-handed magician? He took sleight-of-hand so literally. . . .

My head swam with these thoughts, and I missed my cue. Nick had the next knife solidly inside his overcoat before I remembered to tap the toe button. The knife handle popped out awkwardly. The audience was silent. I'd committed one humdinger of a flub.

I suppose the argument here could be made: *But aren't you hoping that your father will be fired anyway? Was this not your intention?* Well, yes, but even I'm not so callous as to ambush him while he's already bleeding.

The theater manager, who sat in the orchestra pit, held up a sign that said, BEAT IT. My chin fell to my chest.

We'd been kicked offstage for the day.

This had never happened to Nick and me before. Normally, we'd do the show four times in a single day, and here we were, getting ousted during the matinee. That meant a whole day of pay—*pow!*—disappeared.

Nick and I took two quick bows and shuffled offstage. Backstage, I grabbed his injured hand and poked at the wound. He winced.

"We've got to get you to a doctor," I said.

"I'm all right."

"But—"

"I'm fine," Nick sighed deeply and withdrew his hand. "But, Hope?"

"Yes?"

"No more mistakes, understand? I get it."

My heart stilled. "You do?" *He knows he's about to be fired, and that I'm such an awful daughter that I not only didn't tell him, but I perhaps even assisted?*

"You want a day to go visit your Chicago friends."

Pardon?

"Well, now, you've got it, Hopeful. A whole free day. Go visit the old neighborhood, see your pals, what have you. But tomorrow, I'd like to make a fresh start."

Guilt flooded through me and I nodded. "Yes, sir."

Nick chuckled like I'd just said the funniest thing. "How many times do I have to tell you that we're equals here, Hopeful?" He squeezed my shoulder with his good hand. "No 'sir' or 'Dad' or 'Father' around here. Just Nick. Equals, through and through."

I sighed. "You got it."

I hitched a ride on a laundry carriage across town to my old neighborhood, but not to see my friends—because, honestly, I'd been gone five years, and I hadn't kept in touch. I doubt they'd remember or recognize me. No, I was going to conduct a little business.

I didn't ask Nick to go with me. I'd considered it, but I knew he'd decline. I couldn't imagine him strolling along the streets of our old neighborhood, *la-di-da,* as though nothing had happened there. Still, I wished he were with me. Maybe then, a memory or two of my mother would slip loose from his clamped-tight lips.

I sat atop a mound of clean, folded laundry, and the horse trudged through the now-bustling streets of downtown Chicago. Taxis and horseless carriages and even a policeman patrolling on a motorcycle zipped around this tired old mare and her haul, but her progress was steady and reliable. The din of iron wheels on cobblestone streets was near deafening, but welcome. It was approaching dusk, and a breeze drifted off Lake Michigan, a breeze with just enough ice beneath it to send a shiver down my spine. The combination of clean laundry and icy breeze was delicious.

My nerves grew flittery up there on that pile of laundry as we drew closer to my old street. No, no one here would know me. And if they did, I would say I was visiting, um. . . . No. They won't recognize me.

I flipped the driver a jitney when we arrived in Hyde Park. Across from me stood John W. Thompson's General Store, exactly as I remembered it: a crumbling building with drooping awnings and crooked window blinds. The old house was likely a real dandy in its day: a cupola carved a majestic roofline, and a lovely window seat overlooked the corner. A few two-by-fours, a fresh coat of paint, some curtains—that place could be a real home. *A real home.*

Could I actually *do* this? Continue to sell anti-comet pills? It seemed both implausible and, what—immoral?—relying on the desperation of others to make money.

But Nick was to be fired. So, yes, I had to do this. We'd

need money until we could both find jobs. I'd sell pills only until I had enough money to support us for a few weeks. Then I'd stop.

The bell over the door jangled as I entered. "One minute!" a voice croaked from the back room. The candy, as I recalled, was at the back of the store. I weaved through teetering piles of feed and seed toward the rear counter. Among the candy display sat two boxes of Sen-Sen mints. That wouldn't be enough.

An ancient old man, who had probably already died and no one had bothered to tell him, tottered out from a storage area. It couldn't be—Mr. Thompson was still *alive*? He was practically eating dirt the last time I was here. He smacked his gums when he saw me, and his wrinkled face fell open with a *pop!* I thought he might call me by my name.

"Well, hello there, young thing!" he shouted. "What can I do you for?"

He didn't recognize me. I was surprised that I felt saddened by this. It's actually a good thing he didn't recognize me. The last time I was here, he'd caught me stuffing a side of bacon in my knickers. It made for a slippery escape.

"Do you have any more mints?"

"What's that, missy?" The dusty fellow tugged on his earlobe, and the tuft of hair in his ear danced like a tiny rabbit.

I held up the box of Sen-Sen mints. "Do you have any more of these, Mr. Thompson?" I shouted, over-mouthing the words in case he needed to read my lips.

"Call me Jack."

I felt both happy and sad at that. Happy, because I'd known this man my whole life and was honored to address him by his first name. So few adults allowed such an intimacy. But sad, too, because he didn't *know* what an honor he was granting me—to him, I was just another kid off the street.

"Do you have more Sen-Sen mints, Jack?"

"Why, yes, yes, I do. Wait right here a minute. . . ." He teetered around the corner, and I strolled over to the dime novels, cheered by the misadventures of Pluck and Luck. That Pluck! If there's trouble to be had, he steps right in it.

"Here you go, missy," Jack said. He emerged from his storeroom with a small crate of Sen-Sen mints. "How many you need? Two? Three?"

There must've been three dozen tins—hundreds of individual mints. "I'll take them all."

Jack's face lit up, and I could tell he hadn't had a sale this big in weeks. "The whole crate? That'll be . . ." He did the math in his head. "Two dollars." He smiled at me, and his gums glistened in the dim light.

"I can pay $1.25."

Jack scratched his whiskery chin, pulling the loose skin around his mouth to and fro. "For you, Mary, I'll do it."

Mary? Does he think I'm . . . But Jack had already turned to his ledger and was carefully tallying up the day's totals, complete with this latest windfall. I swallowed the question stuck in my throat and began counting out a dollar and a quarter, all hard-earned from my faithful Coins.

This had better be worth it, I thought, watching my money pile up on Jack's side of the counter. *Or else I'm stuck with a lifetime supply of "breath perfume."*

Jack's eyes slid across the countertop with each quarter I

tallied. "Don't see your parents much anymore," he said, as if he were merely commenting on the weather. My throat clenched, and I looked up at him. He didn't seem to be making some sarcastic comment about the death of my mother and the subsequent disappearance of my father and me. No, he thought I was someone named Mary. He meant *her* parents. And surely we weren't talking about the same Mary . . . ?

"Yeah, Tom and Bessie were good customers, Mary. What's become of them?"

But I didn't hear anything further over my swirling thoughts. *Tom and Bessie were my mother's parents. He thinks I'm Mary McDaniels. He thinks I'm my mother.* I lost track of my counting and had to double-check the amount. A difficult task over the thrumming in my ears.

"You still singing up at McCreary's on Fridays? Wish I could get up there to hear you more often."

My mother was a singer? My mind raced backward, and I could suddenly hear lovely notes of "Auld Lang Syne" ringing in the new century. How did I not remember that before?

"You should tour with one of those vaudeville shows, Mary. You're good. A performer at heart." He smiled his toothless grin.

"Here you are, Jack," I said, scooting the pile of money closer to him. I hefted the crate of mints onto my hip. "It's been a pleasure."

"Wait up, Mary!" Jack leaned over the counter and pulled the Pluck and Luck dime novel from its rack. "Take it. I remember how much you love comics."

That he remembered. I'd almost forgotten something so

huge—my mother loved to sing—and Jack Thompson remembered her love for comics. I nearly cried right then at what a cheat our memories really are.

I wished I had a father who mentioned his dead wife *occasionally*, so that I wouldn't have to rely on the memories of strangers. The apology flooded through me: *I'm sorry, Mama. I'm sorry I forgot you loved to sing.*

Sorry: The thought had washed through my veins so often, it was no longer a distinct word, but a feeling.

The door jangled as I opened it for my exit. The old geezer smacked his gums and waved. "Pleasure's all mine, Mary!"

Hearing that again—me, called Mary—I somehow knew then that I was going to pull this off. It was a sign. I was actually going to get away with selling anti-comet pills, and in this crate I held, a thousand tiny talismans awaited their magical destiny. I knew without doubt that this would work.

For I had an angel on my side. An angel, being chauffeured in on a comet.

That night, I couldn't sleep. I ignored the part of my brain that questioned whether my sleeplessness was directly correlated to my first day of selling anti-comet pills. I squashed that voice by reminding myself I'd only do this for a few days, until I had enough money to support Nick and myself for a few weeks after he was released.

I climbed from my bed and crossed the room, the warped floors creaking with every step. Thankfully it did not wake Cross-Eyed Jane. If her own snoring didn't wake her, nothing could.

I wandered from my bedchamber into the hallway of the boardinghouse and looked out the dingy little window. I tried to avoid looking immediately at the comet, but how could one resist? It was now as large and fiery in the night sky as the heart of a candle flame. A pea-size ball of light, edges wavery, flickery, indistinct. We'd soon see a tail, the newspapers said.

The black sky leaked out behind it like a thick pool of ink. It looked so deep, I suddenly had the sensation of falling, and I righted myself by leaning on the windowsill.

"There is no end to space," I'd once read. I felt that now. No end.

May 6, 1910

TWELVE DAYS

till the End of the World.

NEWS HEADLINE

Citizens Flock into Chicago, Fear the End of the World

It is next to impossible to get comfortable on a bench. I mean, do you slump? Hang your backside off the back side? Where do your feet go? And how much room must be left between you and the next fellow, especially when the next fellow is spitting pistachio shells on the floor? Sixty-four pistachio shells, to be exact.

The bench on which I sat was in the audience of the Orpheum Palace Theatre, as our show rolled forth onstage. I had seen each of these acts so many times, it sometimes felt as if the characters being portrayed were my acquaintances, and their scenarios, my memories. As if the dialogue in their acts was the dialogue of my own life.

To say that I was bored would be an under-statement. I was more bored than a tree full of termites.

And so here I sat, bored to the point of near numbness and as uncomfortable as the straight man in a comedy duo. And, too, I was full of dread, because I was about to utter the most foul confessions a person could publicly declare. Pseudo-confessions, but still—huck. But Cross-Eyed Jane needed me, and so here I sat.

After my performance with Nick earlier—which, I should report, I didn't flub—I'd conducted a little anti-comet-pill business with Buster and raked in a quick $5.25. (I'd again avoided the topic of him getting a cut, and he never asked.) But the fellow Cross-Eyed Jane had hired to be her stooge in Chicago had arrived drunk. This fellow's job was simple—shout two questions at Jane as she whirled and twirled about the stage, peddling her elixirs. But there was no way the hired hand could bolster her act as tanked as he was. So Jane planted him in front of a pot of coffee and sent word to me on the beach that I'd have to be her fill-in stooge for the first show. I hated being Jane's fill-in more than I hated being a magician's assistant, but I owed her after I'd suddenly and mysteriously stopped reading tarot cards with her.

I'd returned to the theater after intermission, when I saw all the ladies and gentlemen who'd been smoking long, thin cigarettes outside toss them on the sidewalk and extinguish them with their fancy shoes. I'd filed into the theater and taken my seat, while the chasers cleaned up the last remnants of rotten fruit tossed at the Cherry Sisters and their unbelievable yowling—erm, *singing.*

The first act after intermission was Chekhov's animal act: A group of dogs entered a doggy saloon and bellied up to the two-foot-high bar. After boozing it up on beer mugs full of yellow-tinted water, the pups staggered about the stage, bumping into and falling over one another. One unlucky doggy swaggered into the "street" where a policeman—Happy the Monkey—sat in wait. The promiscuous pup was dragged to the pokey, and the audience howled with laughter.

Next up: Madame Bert Savoy. I suppose if Bert knew French a little better, he'd be Mademoiselle Bert, as it is quite doubtful that the old fellow will ever marry. It was next to impossible to tell that he was a he. Bert was forever trying to give me makeup tips and persuade me to pierce my ears, much to Cross-Eyed Jane's chagrin.

The audience shook their heads and murmured every time Bert took the stage:

"*That* is a gentleman?"

"I'd swear on my mother's grave that that is a lady. If Ma was dead . . ."

And always: "There you go, Bob! Your new gal pal!" This one was always accompanied by a slap on someone's shoulder with a rolled-up program.

Yeah, Madame Bert was every bit woman, except for the bits that count.

And then Cross-Eyed Jane took the stage, and I swam in dread. She tinged and clacked a pair of finger cymbals as she spun tales of the decrepit souls who had dragged themselves to her, only to depart with a twinkle in their eye and a spring in their step. I would've taken notice of her impressive sales techniques, except that all I wanted to do was ooze onto the sticky, pistachio-covered floor and dissipate before I became the stooge.

"She needs a baby? Try taking a little of my St. John's wort, fellas! He's got plantar warts? Buy your man some cantharidin, ladies! You got ills, ailments, disorders, diseases, morbidities? I have the cure-all you need."

That was it. That was my cue. But I just couldn't bring myself to utter Those Words.

Jane twirled, her layers of skirts twittling in circles while she stalled. "Yes, folks, I have the cure for you!"

I cleared my throat. *Here we go.*

"Do you have anything to cure uncontrollable flatulence?"

There. I said it. Everyone around me tilted away, and the pistachio eater finally gave me the girth I preferred. But I wasn't done yet.

"I sure do!" Jane said, twirling over to one of her brown bottles and holding it aloft. "What else, folks? I can make you new again!"

I smacked my lips and sucked in a sharp breath. Might as well get this over with.

"How about loose stools?"

"Absolutely! Why, right here I have . . ."

But her words slammed into background noise as I saw someone peeking from behind the curtain. Buster Keaton.

Of course. The Three Keatons were up next. Somehow, I'd

conveniently forgotten that when I'd agreed to be Jane's substitute stooge.

If embarrassment was deadly, I'd be sporting a toe tag this very moment.

But then I looked closer. Were those . . . ? Yes, those *were* *teeth*. Mr. Stone Face was *smiling*. Awkwardly and uncomfortably, but smiling nonetheless. My own face pulled into a grin of triumph.

I made Buster Keaton smile.

I forgot how uncomfortable I'd been on this bench up till now, and my desire to escape the nearby folks who now viewed me as suspect disappeared. I wanted to watch the Three Keatons.

I'd never seen their act before. They'd only been on the small-small-time circuit for a couple of weeks, and performers are usually loathe to watch another's act—only joke stealers and the overly competitive do that. Plus, Joe and Myra Keaton— Buster's parents—made me uncomfortable to the point of itchiness. They embodied indulgence. Myra, especially. Piles of hair, pounds of makeup—perfectly terrifying.

And the perfume! Myra Keaton wore so much perfume, when she paused, she puddled!

Anyone who spent that kind of money on such frivolities was suspect to me. But despite my distaste for their decadence, I decided it was time to see what all the fuss was about.

The curtains swung open, revealing the elaborate set that had been erected behind it during the last two acts. It resembled a construction zone, an incomplete two-story house. Myra Keaton strode in on the arm of her husband, Joe. Even though she was supposed to resemble the Everyday Housewife during this bit, she did not do a good job covering the fact that she was out-and-out glamorous.

Myra swept her arm approvingly over the incomplete house, and one could tell from the merry music the orchestra played that she was very pleased with her home in progress. But the music turned sharply, as did Mrs. Keaton, and she pointed a stern finger first at her husband, then at the pile of timber lying nearby. The wordless message was clear: "Finish my house!"

Joe Keaton nodded, then stuck his fingers into the corners of his mouth and blew a shrill whistle. Buster plodded out from backstage, dressed exactly like his father, down to the bald cap he wore. The crowd laughed at the very sight of him.

The music underlined Joe's already exaggerated movements. He pointed at Buster, then at a pile of wood, then at the incomplete house. Joe nodded; Buster nodded. Then Joe threw a hammer directly at his son. Buster ducked, and the hammer crashed onto the stage behind him.

That was no magic trick. That was a real hammer.

Next, Joe picked up a two-by-four and spun around, looking for his son. Buster ducked, and ducked, and ducked again, just missing a conk on the head each time. The audience giggled, but Buster's face remained stoic.

Joe shook a finger of shame at Buster, then turned and began nailing boards onto the house. Buster stood one step behind his father, mimicking his every move, and it appeared as though Buster would tap Joe's noggin with his hammer. But when Joe whisked about, Buster drooped like a thirsty plant, the very picture of innocence. This happened three, then four times, and the audience laughed through every bit of it.

Myra returned to the stage, hands on hips, toes tapping. Joe blew her a kiss, then shook his head at Buster. He then scampered up the stairs and began work on the second story.

Buster stopped to take a breather, taking a seat in the first-floor window frame and swiping his brow with a handkerchief. Joe, upstairs, took a mighty swing at the frame of the house, and then, without warning, the entire wall of the house rotated in a half-circle. As Buster was seated inside the window frame, he flipped up to the second floor, looking Joe in the eye, hanging upside down, with no supports or braces.

Hys-*terical*! The audience was roaring now. I was, too. It was easier to laugh than to notice the strength that it took for Buster to clutch the inside of a window frame while suspended one story high, upside down.

Joe pushed Buster in the middle of his forehead, and the entire wall, with Buster therein, rotated back into place. Up, down, up, down—the wall rotated five or six times before Buster dismounted dizzily from the window frame. He stood mid-stage, gathering his breath, and Joe, who had now grown visibly perturbed by his shirker of a son, kicked the upstairs wall.

The entire wall crashed to the stage, with Buster standing

in the hole left by the upstairs window. The audience howled with laughter as a now-fuming Joe stomped down the stairs and stalked over to Buster. Joe hoisted Buster by his scruff of hair and the back of his shirt, and tossed him squarely off-stage.

It was so sudden and so violent, and yet it came in the midst of our riotous laughter. One cannot stem the tide of joy that quickly, and so here we were, forced to laugh at this father tossing his son about like a pair of dirty skivvies. It felt awful.

Joe swiped the palms of his hands together, as if dusting hem off, and ran to the other side of the stage, where his wife enveloped him in a huge hug. The music then changed again, signaling the end of the piece, and all three Keatons swarmed to the middle of the stage and accepted their standing ovation.

And here I thought *my* family was nuts.

Thirty minutes later, I stood with my back pressed against a cold wall while forty-some-odd people radiated from me in a throbbing half-moon. The brick of the wall dug into me, biting my skin. I had set up shop on the beach, but far enough away from the other vendors so they wouldn't notice the mob I attracted. Not so smart, in hindsight.

I still refrained from looking my Coins in the eyes. It was too dangerous for me. Because seeing the fear there made me question myself. So it was easier not to look, to leave the Coins anonymous.

"Those pills, missy. We need more of those pills."

"Oh, that blasted comet! I can feel it in me very bones. You must help an old lady, lass!"

"The farmers south of here ain't even planting their crops. What's the point?"

"I read Italy is flooding thanks to Halley's Comet. That thing is releasing nature's fury!"

It was paralyzing, and I struggled to dole out the pills and pocket the money while standing on the tips of my toes, smashed against a wall. I could only do it if I shut my ears and squinted my eyes, so that these scared people looked less like people.

And then, suddenly, Buster was by my side. "Get into lines, folks!" he shouted at the crowd. "C'mon, now. Everyone will get the medicine they need."

At the edge of the crowd, I caught a glimpse of Mrs. Keaton, her arms folded across her chest, her head cocked like a beautiful bird. Her face was blank, yet I could see she knew exactly what was transpiring. My heart clutched.

Buster was still organizing the Coins when Mr. Whitting strolled out of the boardinghouse to our right. His eyes narrowed and he licked his chapped lips. "What is all this?" he shouted above the pushy crowd.

I managed to tuck the tin of mints back into my pocket. Mrs. Keaton flipped her hair and stepped forward.

"No more autographs today, folks," she said. "I am simply *famished*. Joe!" She pushed around the edge of the crowd, who had quieted as if on cue. Mrs. Keaton made her way to

Mr. Whitting and linked her arm through his. "Please, escort me to the dining room. I have some ideas about promoting us in Lansing."

Mr. Whitting was led away by the jabbering cockatiel. Neither he nor Mrs. Keaton looked back. Our business swiftly resumed. Buster stood at my side.

"Your mother . . . ," I said as I doled out a handful of pills to a Negro woman who had a rainbow of wooden beads braided into her hair.

Buster nodded. "Don't worry about her. She won't take you down." He sold three pills to a man in coveralls and pocketed the quarters.

All the courage that had been sucked from me in the last few moments returned. I wouldn't be able to save enough money to rent a house in fourteen days if I started cutting others in. I raised my eyebrows at him. "You can't keep that money."

Buster's eyes were full of question marks. "Pardon?"

I boldly reached forward and grabbed his pants leg, shaking the fabric. The coins inside his pocket jingled. "*That* money. You can't keep it."

His face pulled into tight, flat lines. "I wasn't planning on it." He crammed his hand in his pocket, dug out the quarters, and thrust them at me.

"Let's get on with this!" someone in the crowd yelled.

I took the quarters from the palm of Buster's hand. "What do you want, then? If not a cut?"

His brow crinkled, and at first I thought the sadness there

was for himself, for opportunity lost. Then I realized—the sadness was for me. It had taken me days to coax a smile from him, but just minutes to make him frown.

Buster worried the outer seam of his pants where they were thin and frayed between his thumb and forefinger. He shook his head and pushed his way out through the crowd.

Did he want . . . a friend?

May 7, 1910

ELEVEN DAYS
till the End of the World.

NEWS HEADLINE

Citizens Flocking into Chicago Fear End of the World

Today was a sold-out performance, which meant I could relax during the show. We always did the levitating trick when the house was standing room only. On crowded days, we could get away with sloppier tricks such as those. The fewer people in the crowd, the tighter the trick had to be. Today, every square inch of bench was filled.

I wore the correct costume, the one with the horrible purple ballet flats and the slit in the leg of the pants. This trick was one of my favorites, not just because my comfort level was high, but because I actually got to don pants. The older ladies in the crowd always whispered when I emerged onstage in trousers.

"So believe what you will about *science*," Nick was saying, making an all-too-obvious reference to Dr. Electricity's act. He was pouring a gallon of water back and forth, back and forth between two pitchers. "Believe what you will about cold calculations and educated guesses. You folks know what an educated guess is? *Still a guess!*" As he shouted this, Nick threw the contents of what was expected to be a water-filled pitcher at the front row. It flitted down upon them in the form of confetti. The crowd laughed. Nick soaked up their approval like a sponge.

Nick had been dismissing Dr. Electricity's assertions all week, and Dr. E was really getting steamed. He'd even complained to Whitting about it, and I must admit, I didn't feel sad at the thought of Nick getting himself into trouble without my assistance.

What's worse than a troublemaker? Two troublemakers.

And I have to say, old Dr. Electricity had been a real killjoy to the anti-comet pill business. His lectures of late had addressed the theories of the world's greatest scientists and how they prophesized no harm to Earth upon the passing of Halley's Comet. So Nick, now taking the "opposite" side of the argument, was doubly beneficial to me.

"Now folks, I'm not saying that we're going to die a fiery death, or be poisoned by leeching gasses, or be smashed into oblivion through contact with this comet," Nick said. He nodded at me, and I readied myself for the finale, the levitating trick. "But those scientists would have you believe that we must clutch our newspapers, hanging on to their every word, anxiously awaiting their next round of calculations. Oh, the power!

"I will say this—do you think we have no control? Do you think we must sit idly by, letting the *scientists* dictate our actions? No! And no! And no again! The mind of man is a powerful thing. And many minds, focusing together, can *alter the cosmos*!"

As Nick was getting all worked up, I slipped my black-socked right foot out of my sewn-on shoe and through the slit in the pants. Then I merely stepped up on a small crate resting on the stage before me, the crate having been painted brown, the same color as the floor of the stage (we did this in each new city). It was surprisingly well camouflaged to the audience. I then balanced atop the crate on my freed right foot. My back was to the crowd, and the fake right foot appeared to hover fifteen inches off the ground, just beside my also-hovering, real left foot.

"So focus, folks! I urge you to focus! Together, we can steer this comet gently away from our home. Together, through nature, with nature, we can *soar*!" Nick threw his arms at me in the grandest of gestures. The crowd wailed in a heady combination of entertainment and what seemed to be relief—relief that they could indeed *do* something about this comet. They could indeed alter the cosmos!

"This comet is a jewel on Mother Nature's necklace! Let us welcome such a thing of beauty! Let us train it with our focused, positive energy!"

It was the first standing ovation we'd received in the five

years we'd been touring. Nick and I took six, then seven bows before bounding offstage.

Backstage, Nick hugged me to his broad chest. "Looks like we've found our gold mine, Hopeful: Halley's Comet!"

Indeed.

I hadn't seen Buster since he walked away from me, frowning, the day before. I'd searched for him between my performances, but to no avail. I had a feeling he'd be absent from my anti-comet pill sales today, so I decided to set up shop behind the theater, with hopes that Whitting wouldn't stumble upon my transactions.

Once I'd recruited a handful of my regular customers on the beach, I herded them into the back alley. Behind the theater, the crowd of pill purchasers was smaller and slightly more manageable. It was less money, yes, but after yesterday's throbbing crowd, I was too intimidated to handle that beast solo.

I stood near the Negro entrance at the rear of the performance hall, trading mints for money. Every once in a while, I allowed myself to open my ears to what my Coins were saying:

"I've built a subcell under my home and will spend the night of the eighteenth underground. Stocked with enough food and water for three months, that dugout."

"You gone to your priest yet, Richard? No? Heavens, boy, you gotta get to confession before this comet streaks by!"

"My daughter gets so mad at me when I tell her she's got to get prepared. I tells her, 'You can't believe them scientists!

Whadda they know?' but she says the newspapers wouldn't print it if it weren't true."

To my right, a fellow troupe member, Hubert Williams, was corking up before his performance. It was still easier not to look my Coins in the eyes (because then they'd become *people,* of course), so I watched Hubert as he lit a piece of cork on fire, puffed out the flame, and then smeared ashes over his already-dark skin.

Many of the actors performed in blackface, even the Negro performers, like Mr. Williams. When we first joined the circuit, I had asked Nick why a Negro person would smear black makeup on his face. Nick had ranted and raved about the ludicrousness of the tradition of blackface, stabbing the air with a single finger and declaring that this nation was a nation of equals. All right, but that still didn't answer my question. I found out later from Cross-Eyed Jane that management required all Negro performers to wear blackface so they wouldn't scare the almost-always all-white audience. Which seemed both silly and sad.

Mr. Williams shifted his mouth to the far left corner of his face and smeared the burned cork on his right cheek. He didn't use a mirror. As he applied his makeup, he caught my eye.

"Hey, you—the magician's kid!" he called, pulling his collar out from his neck and smearing the cork beneath his neckline.

I glanced at my Coins; I was leery of identifying myself. I shrugged at Mr. Williams.

He sensed that I was withholding information and nodded. "Looks like Whitting doesn't know what you're up to back here."

I swallowed and tried to ignore him. He'd finished with the

cork and tossed it in a nearby rubbish heap. "Listen, just be careful. Whitting hears about you making money and not giving him a cut, things could get real bad for you and your daddy, you hear?"

One could hope.

"I don't just mean getting fired, either. Whitting's got connections. Mean, nasty connections. Don't make him mad, you hear me?"

My throat closed shut to keep my fear trapped in my chest rather than leaking out my eyes. I'd heard rumors about performers "disappearing." Could that really happen?

Mr. Williams left us to our business, entering the theater through the back door.

The woman with the beads in her hair to whom I'd sold pills yesterday stood next to me. "Girl, don't you worry. Somebody comes pickin' on you, they gonna have to get through *us* first." She clamped a dry, wrinkled hand around mine.

My instinct was to jerk my hand away from this stranger, until I looked up into her deep brown eyes. She gave my hand a weak squeeze.

The man in the coveralls, also from yesterday, nodded. "Ain't nobody takin' our hope away."

At first I thought that somehow, this crab apple of a fellow had uncovered my name. Had I not hidden my name on the tin adequately with my thumb? Then I realized: He meant *hope*. Opportunity. Faith.

His eyes were gray-blue, like clouds after a storm. I scanned the faces of my other Coins—Asian eyes, eyes clouded with cataracts, eyes wide with trust.

Trust. I gave these people hope in a time of desperation. Something to believe in, some form of action to take. They needed me. They needed hope. And Hope.

I reopened the tin. "Now, who here has kids they're buying pills for? Grandkids? You folks get priority. . . ."

That evening after the last performance, all the actors huddled backstage while the chasers cleaned up the last remnants of rubbish from the day's attendees. The crew scurried between the benches, sloshing buckets of brown water onto the concrete floor and pushing it around with gray mops. It smelled like rotting fruit and wet dog.

Whitting had called an emergency meeting at the theater. All performers were required to attend. These emergency meetings could be anything from a true emergency—"Williams's gallstones are acting up again, so we got to shuffle the bill to cover for him"—to things that Whitting considered an emergency: "I lost a gold filling from my tooth earlier today. Any of you shysters seen sticking that hunk of gold in your grouch bag will be done."

Yeah, old man Whitting was so cheap, he couldn't even pay attention.

Cross-Eyed Jane stood next to me, her arm draped casually about my shoulders. She was leaning on me kind of heavy, but I didn't mind the extra weight. She looked tired. If I felt awful about anything I'd done these last few days, it was leaving her to fend for herself with the tarot cards. But she'd seemed fine when I told her I was taking a break from doing the readings. "Stop apologizing!" she'd said. "Everybody has to stop running so fast at some point."

Exactly.

Whitting stood on an orange crate and clapped his hands to get our attention. I balanced on tiptoe and scanned the room to see where Buster stood, but I couldn't find him.

"All right, folks, settle down. Hush, now. It has come to my attention that some of our performers have been capitalizing on this whole comet thing."

Every muscle in my body felt instantly frozen. Could he mean me? I searched the room and finally locked eyes with Buster. It was impossible to tell what that fellow was thinking behind that stone face of his.

"I understand that today, Nick and his assistant got their first standing ovation," Whitting said. He clapped his thick hands in our general direction. "Huh, folks? How about that? Number three on the bill gets a standing ovation!" The other performers weakly tapped their fingers into the palms of their hands, giving us our due. Nick smiled and popped a handful of mints into his mouth and crunched them loudly.

I shrugged at Buster and smiled extra wide. *Guess we're okay,* my gesture said. Buster's head turned back to Whitting, as if he hadn't seen me.

"So here's what we're gonna do, folks. We only got this comet in our sights for the next coupla days. Let's milk this cow. I want each and every one of you to find a way to incorporate Halley's Comet into your acts."

The performers let out a collective groan. I couldn't say I blamed them.

"Impossible!" Joe Keaton shouted. He swayed and took a swaggery step forward. "That comet has nothing on the Three Keatons!"

Whitting shook his head so violently, I thought it might propel right off his neck. "No, no, not you, Joe. The Three Keatons are exempt."

Mr. Keaton's face pulled into a smug smile, and he stepped back into the crowd. I thought Whitting might jump off his box and lick Joe Keaton's boots clean.

"But the rest of you!" Whitting said, and pointed a finger down at us all. "Do it! This comet is a novelty, and the element of novelty is the essence of vaudeville.

"We've been standing still," he continued. "And whatever is standing still is going backward. Or at least other things are passing it. So put in one lousy comet. No complaints, or you're done."

Whitting hopped off the box and plucked a cigar from his breast pocket. The meeting was apparently finished. The performers grumbled and made their way to the exits.

I weaved through the crowd and found Buster. "Guess we're okay," I whispered.

Buster stopped in the midst of the pushing crowd. "We?" he asked.

The performers continued to push forward all around him, like water around a rock. I was trapped in the stream, and I got dragged away.

Whatever is standing still is going backward.

Not always.

May 8, 1910

TEN DAYS

till the End of the World.

NEWS HEADLINE

Experts in Doubt as to Effect of Comet on Earth

Nick had told me over a bowl of cold porridge that we'd be performing Head Twister as our finale today. *Head Twister,* I had thought. *How apt.*

So now I stood onstage, dressed in a musty red-orange-and-yellow-striped dress that Nick had dug from the depths of an old costume trunk. "The colors of the comet!" he'd said, almost in a squeal. It was pinned and tucked into a silhouette that was slightly more flattering than an elephant's hide.

Head Twister, despite its awful name and the effect of the trick itself, was child's play compared to some of the other tricks. With a flourish, Nick introduced the Head Twister box to our audience, a box comprised of steel girders and two large clamps. The box appeared to be open on all sides, resembling the cubes that mathematics students are taught to sketch to give the effect of three dimensions.

Nick situated the box over my head like my very own personal halo, with my face peering through one of the openings in the grid.

"About this comet," he said, jiggling the massive clamps, knocking on the steel girders. "Let's get our heads on straight."

The crowd giggled. And *pow*! They were primed.

Nick twisted the mighty clamps on both sides of the box. The clamps screwed in, tighter and tighter, until they hugged both sides of my skull. Members of the audience began to murmur as they assumed that my head would pop if Nick continued tightening the clamps.

Head Twister? That trick is such a headache.

"You know," Nick said, "there are other comets—bigger and wilder comets—that visit us for a while and go off, never to return."

Nick continued tightening. Or so it appeared. He stood to my left, grunting and grumbling, pretending to have much difficulty with those pesky clamps. In actuality, he was not tightening the clamps, but adjusting a series of hidden mirrors inside the box.

"One of these days, perhaps a million years from now, or on May eighteenth, one of these great bodies might strike the Earth and destroy us."

As Nick appeared to struggle with the massive screws, I turned my head inch by inch to the right, giving the illusion that my head was rotating completely backward within the box under the force of the clamps.

"But if a comet did strike us, we should not know it! We should never even have time to *think* about it! And, sad to relate, neither we little Earth dwellers nor our solar system would be missed in the vast cosmic mechanism in which suns, planets, comets, and nebulae play their part!"

When the series of mirrors reflected the back of my head attached to the front of my body, Nick leapt aside and threw his arms toward me in a sidewise V. I believe he expected the audience to jump to their feet and applaud madly, as they had done yesterday, but they most certainly did not. How could they? He had just told this crowd that if Halley's Comet were to strike us, tiny little Earth would not even be missed!

It was a mistake for me to talk while in the Head Twister contraption, because moving might've given away the mirrors and how the trick worked. But I did, anyway.

"Hope," I murmured to my father.

Beads of sweat had popped up on his brow. He swallowed and glanced at me, apparently wondering why I might be saying my own name at this extremely awkward moment. I crinkled my eyebrows at him, too afraid to attempt speaking again.

Give them hope, my eyes pleaded.

Nick's show-business smile transformed almost imperceptibly into his real smile. He got it.

"But who among us truly *believes* that? That we're just a tiny target hurtling through the vast universe? That we have no purpose, no path?" And then Nick did something he'd never done before. He started performing the Head Twister trick in reverse. We'd never practiced this; the trick usually ended with

Nick leading me offstage with the box still atop my shoulders, my head still crooked.

I inched my head to the left, synchronizing my movement with Nick's as best I could. He emphasized to our audience how difficult these clamps were to loosen.

"Our current purpose, as I see it, is to shoo this pesky comet from our doorstep. I truly believe that even the lowest among us has the ability to do this, but"—he appeared to struggle with the clamps here, and I thought he might actually fumble this trick—"But! We, the citizens of planet Earth, united, are unstoppable! Unrestrainable! Infallible! Indestructible!"

My head was forward-facing again; or rather, it appeared this way to our now—wildly applauding audience. It had actually been facing in the correct direction the whole time, but of course no one knew this.

"So get your head on straight, folks!" Nick shouted. "Open your minds and drive this comet skyward with sheer will power! We can do this! United, we can!"

I had to turn my whole body sidewise to look at Nick, as the Head Twister contraption still rested upon my shoulders. But I knew—*could feel*—how much he believed what he was saying. He was doing it. He was Altering the Cosmos.

And so was his howling, cheering audience.

Behind the Orpheum Theatre, anti-comet pills sales were brisk, despite the fact that cats picked through the piles of rubbish next to us, looking for more than just empty tins of tuna, I assumed. Ten or twelve of my same Coins had been here yesterday. I realized that this made me happy, and not because I'd managed to establish a regular clientele. No, it made me happy because I was important to these people. Or, at least my pills were.

> **Did you hear the one about the guy who thought he was so important, he looked down his nose at everyone? Yeah, he drowned in a thundershower.**

Huck. I shook off my distraction. "Thank you," I said, selling three pills to a man leaning on a carved mahogany walking stick. The stick was amazing, a tower of skulls and bones stacked in a neat pile. "Thank you."

"Thank *you*, missy," he said with a wink of a blue eye. "You're doing a good thing here."

I swallowed a gulp of air, which pushed aside a swell of guilt, and smiled weakly at him. "I like helping people."

"It shows," he said, and teetered away on his skeleton stick.

A woman wearing piles of ill-fitting clothes and stacks of fake jewelry jingled up next. "I brought you something, girlie," she said, reaching into her overstuffed carpetbag.

I shook my head. "No, ma'am, I'm sorry. I can't barter. Cash only."

The bejeweled lady smiled at me; her teeth were surprisingly straight and brilliant white. "I got my quarters, missy. No worries." She dug around in her purse and pulled out a piece of crumpled paper—a program from our vaudeville show. Inside the paper was a greasy, crumbly chicken leg. I hadn't had chicken in months. The meals at the boardinghouses and on the railcars hardly qualified as meals. My mouth watered.

"You looked a little peaked. Doesn't the girlie get enough to eat?"

I shook my head, then realized what she'd asked, and nodded. "Yes, ma'am. I'm fine. No thank you for the chicken," I heard myself say. But my stomach betrayed me and grumbled.

The woman threw her head back and laughed, and her jewelry swayed and jingled. "Take it. If you don't, I'll feed it to those undeserving varmints," she said, pointing at the cats with the toe of her boot.

I couldn't take that chicken, could I? If there was one rule that was hard and fast on our small-small-time circuit, it was not to befriend the townies. Sure, I was breaking all sorts of unwritten rules with these pills—not giving Whitting a cut being the main one—but that "no fraternizing with the townies"? That rule was sacred. Everyone obeyed that one.

But I was hungry. So I nodded and tucked the chicken leg into my pocket. Suddenly I could think of nothing but.

"My pills?" the lady asked. She had three quarters in the palm of her extended hand.

"Oh, yes. Yes, of course!" I exchanged pills for quarters and continued business. "C'mon, folks, don't be shy," I said to the rest of my customers. "We can beat this comet yet!"

A small cheer rose from the handful of people still purchasing pills. I smiled. A pocket full of jingly quarters and dinner that wasn't succotash. A good day. Not perfect, but now, at least, I let myself imagine that a perfect day was within grasp.

I sprawled on my squeaky cot in the boardinghouse, still licking the salt from my fingers from the delicious chicken leg. The cracks in the plaster ceiling resembled train tracks, crossing this vast nation. I blinked and tried to make them look like a house instead.

Cross-Eyed Jane came into the room and drooped onto her cot. She kicked off her shoes, and soon the whole room smelled like feet. Surely she must have a cure for that in her bag of elixirs?

"Good day?" I asked.

She nodded. "And how's about her with them pills, lovey?"

I tensed and bolted upright. But Cross-Eyed Jane's face stretched into a huge smile.

I blinked. "How did you find out?"

She pulled off a clip earring. "Lovey, she's gotta be real careful, hear?"

I nodded. *Mrs. Keaton,* I thought. *She told.* "You want in?" I asked. I thought it would pain me to ask that, but it didn't. With Jane, I could share.

She took off a sweaty scarf and flipped me with the tail. "Naw. She's saving up for something big."

I laughed. "And how do you know *that?*"

She shrugged. "I know my lovey would cut me in otherwise." She looked at me with one eye, the other eye wandering up to those plaster cracks. "She *would,* right?"

It wasn't a threat. It was a question from someone whose heart was a little tender right now.

I nodded and lay back down on my cot. It moaned. In my head, I calculated how much money I might need to take Jane off the circuit with us. I doubted she'd come if I asked, though— vaudeville was as much a part of Jane as her very bones.

Jane snuffed out the lantern light. There were no windows in this tiny room, so the only light crept in under the door. Probably for the best; otherwise it might be difficult to get a good night's sleep in this joint.

"I read the cards for her today, lovey," Jane said. Though I couldn't see if she was addressing me in this dark room, I assumed "her" meant me. I never believed in the cards, but Jane did.

"Yeah?"

"Yes. Her future looks solid. She got the Wheel of Fortune card."

"Ooo! I'm going to be wealthy?" I asked with a chuckle.

Jane laughed, too. "Not always. More often, the Wheel of Fortune has to do with destiny or fate. Superior forces, see? Movement?"

I thought of Nick and his pleas to our audience to help him move the comet through sheer will power. Impossible. Right?

"Jane?" I asked. I was tired, but I'd wanted to ask her this question all day.

"Yep?"

"How do you get a friend who's mad at you to stop being mad at you?"

"Tell 'em sorry, lovey."

"That's it? Really?"

Jane yawned loudly. "And mean it."

"Okay. I'm sorry I stopped reading tarot cards, Jane."

"Mmm-hmm. But I'm not the one who needs the apology, lovey. If I had to guess, it's that right smart Keaton fella. No?"

I smiled into the darkness. And how could she know *that*?

Maybe she saw it in the cards.

May 9, 1910

NINE DAYS

till the End of the World.

NEWS HEADLINE

Whole World Waits Comet's Tail as It Sweeps Earth

I found Buster in the least likely place of all: in the audience of the Orpheum Palace Theatre. His long, lean frame was easy to spot in the darkened performance hall.

> **Buster Keaton? That fellow was so thin, the crease in his pants was him!**

He sat hunched forward, his boots propped on the bench in front of him, his elbows on his knees. His sitting like that, so awkwardly, made me uncomfortable. Or perhaps the fact that I was spying on him caused my discomfort.

Winsor McKay was onstage, delivering his chalk talk. McKay sketched five separate illustrations simultaneously, darting back and forth between large pads of paper propped on easels and telling humorous stories that related to the drawings. The pictures looked like mere scribbles at first, but with each pass of McKay's pen, they came into focus. The bit was hilarious, the audience loved it, but Buster sat hunched over, nodding his head and studying McKay's drawings with gleaming eyes.

I worked up the courage to sit down next to him. "He's good," I said, jerking my head at the stage.

Buster nodded, still watching McKay. "How do you think he does that? Draws five pictures at once?"

I shrugged and smiled to myself, not a little surprised that he'd even talk to me. "Lots of practice, I suppose."

He turned to me. "Yeah, but one picture is hard enough. I mean, he even has backgrounds and different perspectives in each sketch. Do you know how difficult that is?"

His eyes were wide and soft, and my breath caught in my chest. I shook my head.

Then his eyes hardened, and Buster looked as if he suddenly remembered that he was angry with me. He turned back to McKay's bit.

I leaned toward him. He smelled like sawdust and soap. "I'm sorry," I whispered.

Buster looked at my knees, and my knees have never felt such scrutiny in all their thirteen years.

"Really. I am an awful person," I continued, and giggled. Giggled! Me! Nerves, I suppose. "I could make a list of all my indiscretions, if you'd like. Would you prefer alphabetical order, or in order of severity?"

His face twitched into a grin. "Let's get out of here."

Faint. "And go where?"

His eyes lit up like stage lights. "Let's go to a nickelodeon!" he said. He grabbed my hand and pulled me toward the exit. Okay, let's be honest. Not really *pulled*. I went willingly.

I'd never been to a moving picture show, and I wanted to go, but I shook my head. "There's not time," I said, blinking as we pushed onto the sunny sidewalk. "You're on in two hours."

"Sure there's time," Buster said, dropping my hand. It suddenly felt all cold and lonely. "*If* we take a car . . ."

I knew from the devilish gleam in Buster's dark eyes that he didn't mean we should catch a taxi. He strode toward the boardinghouse, behind which sat Whitting's Model T.

"C'mon," he said over his shoulder, not even looking to see if I'd follow. "What's one more indiscretion on the list?"

I followed.

Did you hear the one about the guy who had money to burn? He lit his cigars with twenty-dollar bills.

Yep, old Whitting kept a car in Chicago for the handful of days a year our troupe was in the city. What a waste. I shuddered to think of how else that money could've been used, who that money could've helped. Because there were plenty of people who needed money for Very Important Things. I knew that all too well. So I didn't really feel all that guilty when Buster and I hopped into Whitting's green Flivver.

Buster dug around in the car, looking for the key. He found it, predictably enough, stowed under the front seat. "Aha!" he said, dangling it before me.

"And why do you get to drive?" I asked. As much as I hated what this car stood for, I sure wouldn't mind taking it for a spin. Even though I'd never driven before.

Buster pointed to the steering wheel and raised his eyebrows at me in a way that made my stomach flitter. I looked to where he pointed. MEN AND BOYS ONLY, read a gold placard attached to the wheel. Huck. That Whitting.

"Well, if you're going to drive, you're certainly going to need *these*," I said, twisting around my seat to retrieve a horrid pair of driving goggles resting in the backseat. They dangled off my finger. Buster smirked and leaned toward me, allowing me permission to put the goggles on for him. My hands shook as I stretched the goggles over his brown hair, and I snapped the back of his head with the leather band.

"Ow!"

"Sorry." I lifted the thick, black circles of the eye holes and placed them over his eyes. He looked like a bug. A bug with bad eyesight. I spat out a laugh.

"Well, I think I look splendid," Buster said, pulling a side-view mirror toward him. "But *this* . . ." He reached in the back and retrieved a white driving smock, like the ones doctors or scientists wore. "This really completes the look, no?" He put the too-large smock over his flannel shirt and struck a pose, dangling his wrist casually over the steering wheel. He looked just like those sporty drivers pictured in the newspapers: ridiculous.

"I'll say." I covered my mouth with my hand for fear of him seeing me smile too much. My daffy giveaway grin. Heaven help me, I was *grinning* at the boy. Where did this come from?

"Hang on," he said, hopping out and cranking the engine with the hand crank. He jumped back in, unlocked the steering wheel with the key, and squeezed the rubber bulb of the horn twice.

"Flickers, here we come!" he said.

Five minutes later, we slammed to a stop before the Granada Theatre. Buster was a horrible driver. Just awful. Stops and starts, stalls and fitful gear shifts. I hopped out of the car before he'd even cut the engine.

"Either you let me drive home or I'm hitching," I said, dusting off my skirts.

"You? Drive?" Buster laughed. "Sure. But if we get caught, wouldn't it be better for Whitting to see me driving than you?"

Good point.

We crossed the cobblestone street to the moving picture house. I found myself hesitating before entering the nickel-odeon theater. The theater itself was grandish, bordering on garish, covered in colorful paintings depicting scenes from the stories it was now throwing. Scenes of ladies in poofy dresses swooning over mustached males. Scenes of cherubs, gazing with golly-gee cheeks to the pale pink skies of heaven. Scenes of a Tin Lizzy zipping across railroad tracks as a steam loco-motive barreled toward it.

"This is my treat," I said, as we approached the ticket booth. Yes, I admit, I had to squash the dread of spending an entire dime so frivolously. But I needed to do this to demonstrate how sorry I was.

"Yes, it is, kid," Buster said, stepping aside and gesturing to the ticket window.

Kid. I paused before purchasing our tickets. Organ music blared onto the walkway, enticing visitors to fork over the five cents and come inside. Electric lights hung like a glorious strand of pearls above the entryway. And of course, the interior was likely dim, and the chairs were likely intimately positioned, and here I was, with a gentleman friend, without a chaperone. Still, my pet name from this gentleman friend was *kid.*

As if reading my mind, Buster tugged at my sleeve. "Watching a flicker with a friend is no worse than selling anti-comet pills," he said. "Come on."

He strode forward, pulling me by my elbow toward a red velvet curtain. We dropped our tickets into the chopping box and ducked inside.

The interior of the theater was indeed dim, and the walls bore a burgundy hue, which made the small room feel even more crowded. Signs dotted the walls, similar to the ones that welcomed our vaudeville crowds: NO SMOKING; HATS OFF; STAY AS LONG AS YOU LIKE. The chairs—yes, they were chairs, not benches—were a mishmash of old kitchen furniture, and after we found two empty seats, Buster grabbed the empty chair in front of him, spun it around, and propped his boots upon it.

Also like our vaudeville show, the moving picture ran continuously throughout the day, so it was already rolling when we entered. And while I'd heard them called "flickering flicks," I was unprepared for the rapid flickering of lights that accompanied a moving picture being thrown onto a screen. The on-off-on-off lighting gave me the sensation of blinking too quickly. Initially, my head spun with the effort of watching the stories. But my vision slowly adjusted to the movement, and I soon found myself enjoying the follies of a bank robbery gone awry. Buster grinned so large I thought he might actually injure an underused smiling muscle.

In the blue-white dancing light of the theater, Buster and I watched three more fifteen-minute stories: *Romany's Revenge, Wizard's World,* and *Catch the Kid,* a romp of a story that turned out to be a real screamer. Even Buster laughed so hard he choked, and I felt obligated to whack him on the back several times.

> **Did you hear the one about the kid who laughed himself to death? He sure put the fun in funeral. . . .**

The next tale held me spellbound. The story itself was simple—a poor man wished for new clothes. He was ratty, not unlike most of my Coins, and his wish for a new wardrobe was apparent from the overwrought spectacle he made of himself near a wishing well. The organ music grew weepy and weary as the man lay down for a rest. His wish came true, as I suspected it would, but oh, my! The tricks in this bit! The fabric *unrolled itself,* a piece of chalk marked the pattern *by itself,* and then the scissors! The scissors cut the fabric *without aid*! With no one working them! I looked for the props I knew must be guiding these tricks—strings, mirrors, buttons—but found none.

"How are they doing that?" I whispered to Buster. He shrugged and shook his head, as mesmerized as I was. It was the best deceit I had ever witnessed. And I'd witnessed some pretty amazing deceit in my day.

A stretcher film was thrown next, one in which the audience is encouraged to stretch its legs or visit the facilities. The film depicted the landscape from a moving train. Oh, huck. I didn't need to come to a theater to see that; I saw it every week. Patrons around us stood, stretched, and talked about the stories.

The landscape on the picture screen whizzed by, and I watched it numbly. I'd probably seen that very stalk of corn, that very blade of grass. I tried to concentrate on the passing scenery, but I had trouble doing so. Watching land zip by while sitting perfectly still, minus the subtle pull of forward momentum one feels on a train, confused my brain. I started to feel dizzy, even nauseous.

"You know what the problem with that story is?" Buster said.

I shook myself out of my daze. "Pardon?"

"That story—with the scissors? That fellow should've wished for a pile of money, like a thousand dollars or something. Then he could've had lots of new suits. But instead he wishes for one lousy change of clothes? Stupid bit, if you ask me."

He turned, and I could feel him grinning at me. "You'd wish for that, wouldn't you? A pile of money? If you had just one wish?"

A pile of money? As my *only* wish? What kind of person did he think I was? Oh, my. No. He had it all wrong.

He had *me* all wrong.

No, I couldn't have him believing that. I took a deep, wavering breath and shook my head.

"No. If I had just one wish, it'd be to have my mother back."

I looked at him then, and his eyes seemed as deep as tunnels. I lowered my gaze and whispered, "The money would be too late."

When Buster drove Whitting's Model T sputtering and stalling into the parking lot behind the theater, Bert Savoy was there, waving long, lacy-gloved arms at us. Buster nearly mowed over him. We hopped out of the Flivver.

"Girl, Whitting is as mad as a bull!" Bert flittered up to us, straightening my dress on my shoulders, smoothing my hair. Bert's voice was sweet and high-pitched and sometimes hard to hear, it was so squeaky.

"What's that?" Buster asked. Bert shot him a look of vile from beneath his thick black eyelashes.

Bert continued to me, "Cross-Eyed Jane says Whitting's been stomping around here like a toddler, looking for his car. Where have you two been?"

I shrugged and readied myself for Bert's scrutiny, but he yanked Whitting's key out of Buster's hand and shoved him aside.

"Hey!" Buster started, but Bert shushed him with another sharp glare.

"What the hell is going on here?"

I whipped about to see Whitting storming up to our group. My stomach clenched.

"Why, I was just taking your little Flivver here for a spin, Joe." Bert's voice climbed an octave higher, and he batted his thick lashes at Whitting. But beads of sweat broke out on his upper lip.

As odd as it may seem, Bert Savoy was one of Whitting's pet performers. Bert kept to himself, and he made the crowds happy. Whitting narrowed his eyes at Bert, at us.

Bert lifted up the hem of his dress and crossed the dusty lot to Whitting. He pressed the key into Whitting's hand and gave it a squeeze.

"Sorry I didn't get the chance to ask, Joe," he cooed. "It was kind of an emergency. Girl stuff."

Whitting was so flustered at that—what kind of girl emergency could Bert Savoy possibly have!—that he could only stammer, "Don't let it happen again." He quickly inspected his car and stormed off.

Bert whirled around to me. "That was stu-*pid*, girl! You know better. And *you*!" he said, his voice falling into his true, deep man-voice. It always shocked me, Bert using that voice. Like a kitten barking. He placed a long, pink fingernail on Buster's chest. "No funny business."

If I could've disintegrated into the cosmos right then, I would've.

Buster blinked. "Yes, sir. Ma'am. Uh—you got it."

May 10, 1910

EIGHT DAYS
till the End of the World.

NEWS HEADLINE

Will Halley's Comet Harm the Earth?

The mornings were still crisp, and my breath puffed in tiny clouds as Buster and I stood behind the theater, doling out pills before our first performance. My regular customers were there—the lady with the beads in her hair, the gentleman in the coveralls, the fellow with the carved cane, the old lady with the piles of jewelry, the redhead cradling the tiny baby. There were a few Coins I did not recognize that morning, but there was nothing abnormal about that. Many Coins purchased pills once and never returned. I wondered if those Coins thought that one pill was adequate, and a tinge of worry shot through me for their safety.

What was I *thinking*? Of course, one pill was adequate! *No* pill was an adequate defense against Mr. Halley's fiery comet! Huck, this anti-comet pill business really had me going dizzy.

The crowd thinned and departed. One straggling Coin remained on the fringe of the alley, hovering in the space between the theater and the shoe repair shop—HEEL THY SOLE—next door. The sunlight cut between the buildings behind him, so it was impossible to get a read on his shadowy face. I shrugged. Many Coins needed a day or so to work up enough courage to purchase their first pill. He'd come around.

"We ought to get going," Buster said. I nodded, and I huffed on my icy fingers to keep them moving. As I did, Buster bent over to tie his boot strings. As *he* did, I saw it: a flash of knife from the grubby gentleman hovering at the alley's entrance. I caught just enough of a glance of the knife—a rusty, saw-toothed kitchen knife—before he swept up next to me, pinning my right arm painfully behind my back, my left arm to my side. He held the toothy knife to my neck, and it pricked me in three or four distinct points of pain. The pills crashed to the ground and scattered and bounced about the alley. Buster froze in his crouch, fear etched on his face.

"Hold still!" the fellow growled in a Southern drawl. He stank like body odor and rubbish. Being pinned against him was almost worse than the four points of pain on my neck, but I stopped squirming. "Right. This little girlie here is gonna give me the rest of them pills, ain't you, now?"

Buster rose slowly. "Sir, let's be reasonable. . . ."

The smelly dog whipped me around so he could get a better

look at Buster. The pain in my arm made me wince. Buster lifted the palms of his hands.

"Pick 'em up!" the man shouted. "The pills. Pick 'em up or she gets hurt."

Buster began picking up the anti-comet pills from the grubby alley. I shifted slightly, getting my bearings against this nasty creature. He tightened his foul grip.

The straitjacket trick. My arms were tied just like this—well, almost—in the straitjacket trick.

I shifted once more and realized—yes, I had just enough wiggle room to do it. And so I did.

I arched my left foot and shot it straight up behind me— *pow!*—as hard as I could. The heel of my boot landed perfectly in a place that, well, let's just say we don't discuss in polite company.

The dog dropped the rusty knife, and I kicked it aside with the toe of my shoe. My attacker hunched forward from the pain of my kick, and Buster slammed down his elbow on the back of the man's head. The dirty fellow collapsed into the sludge of the alley. Buster placed his boot squarely in the middle of the man's back.

"Go get a police officer," he told me. I nodded and darted through the triangle of sunlight onto the sidewalk, blinking back tears.

Sometimes the stars and the planets align perfectly. A police officer stood a mere half block away, the sun glinting off the brass buttons on his navy uniform.

"We were attacked," I said, running up to him. I kept the

facts to the bare minimum. No need to alert Chicago's finest to the fact that I was peddling anti-comet pills, right?

He followed me back to the alley. Buster still squashed the nasty fellow into the slop of the alley with his boot. The officer hefted my attacker by the scruff of his collar and pinned him against the wall of the theater.

"You attack these here folks?" the officer growled at him. The fellow winced. "Yeah?" the officer asked, pushing him harder against the brick wall. I cast my eyes to the pile of garbage next to the back door.

A low moan started within the attacker, which grew into a long, sorrowful sob. It sounded like the rumble of a train on tracks and felt just as lonely. It came from a place within the dirty fellow that was so hollow, it seemed to echo inside him before it escaped.

"She has the answer!" he wailed. "She can save us from the comet! Her comet pills can save us!"

My muscles tensed so sharply, I felt like the edge of a razor blade.

"Comet pills, eh?" The officer caught the attacker's hands with a pair of silvery handcuffs. He looked over the brass buttons on the shoulder of his uniform and winked at Buster and me. "Right. Got yourself a real loony here, huh, folks?"

Buster swallowed and chuckled. "Yes, sir!"

The officer dragged the ragged, moaning man down the alley, toward the shaft of sunlight. "She has them, officer! Comet pills! She has them!"

"Yeah, right," I heard the officer say before dragging the fellow around the corner of the Heel Thy Sole shoe shop. "And

I got these special gas masks you can buy, see. They'll save your life!"

Only then did my muscles melt. I swiped at the dots of blood on my neck. Not bad, but the sight of my own blood on my fingers made me shake. I wanted to sit down, but everything in the alley was covered with a film of dirt. I leaned against the wall of the theater.

Buster took a handkerchief from his pocket and dabbed my neck with it. Thank goodness I had a valid reason to shake, or else my trembling would've seemed unbearably obvious. He smiled. "Where'd you learn that move, kid?"

I shrugged and managed to choke out, "Stop calling me kid."

He chuckled and looked closer at the cuts on my neck. "Can't you just be a plugger?"

I shook my head and pushed off the wall to standing. "There's not enough money in peddling sheet music, *friend*." I laid thick on the *friend*, with hopes that he'd see that I knew we were just pals, despite my trembling.

I dusted off my skirts and patted my hair. "Business resumes tomorrow!" I said, pretending that I was fine, thank you. Though honestly, I was uncertain I'd be brave enough to continue.

I realized too late that I had not said thank you to Buster for, well, saving me. I cringed at that—*saving me*. He hadn't really *saved* me, right? Just helped. I didn't need someone to rescue me. But it would've been a whole lot messier if he hadn't been there, so I supposed I needed to acknowledge that.

That evening, I spied him at the dinner table at the

boardinghouse. He was pushing a pile of green glop against a pile of brown glop with a spoon.

Honestly, I miss boardinghouse cooking. Every chance I get!

"Don't eat it," I said, dropping into the chair opposite him. I pointed at his gruesome plate and grinned. "I'm rescuing you. Do not eat that."

He dropped his spoon onto his plate with a clang. "Thank you! Who knows what kinds of injuries I might've sustained." Half his face raised in a grin. I had to take a deep breath at that.

"Yeah, well, thank you, too, I guess," I mumbled. I twisted the linen napkin that sat on the table before me into a knot. "You know, for the help earlier."

Buster stuck a knuckle in his ear and jimmied it about. "I'm sorry? Did I just hear Hope McDaniels say *thank you*?"

I tossed the knotted napkin at him. He chuckled.

"I brought you this," I said. I flipped the Pluck and Luck dime novel that my buddy Jack at the general store had given me next to his plate.

"Wow! Thank you!" Buster's eyes lit up like stars. He opened the book and traced his finger over the illustrations, as if studying how they were created.

The next moment passed without us saying a word. As did the next. And the next. I felt myself begin to burn with blush.

Ever hear of a pregnant pause? This pause was so pregnant, it was giving birth!

"I, uh, saw your act, you know?" I stammered at last.

"Yeah?" Buster's eyes shined, and he leaned forward, propping his elbows on the table. "What did you think?"

It's horrible, I wanted to say. *The way they throw you around like that.* But instead I said, "How do they throw you so far?" Huck. How stupid.

"Neat trick, huh? My mom sewed a suitcase handle on the back of my costume. Really helps Dad chuck me far, you know?"

"Doesn't it hurt?"

"Naw. You learn how to fall correctly."

I wished I could learn how to do that. Fall correctly. But again I edited myself. "The crowd really eats it up."

"Yeah. Not everybody likes it, though." He picked up the Pluck and Luck dime novel and flipped through it rapidly, running his thumb over the pages—*zip*!

"Yeah?" *Of course they don't.*

"Yeah. That's actually why we're on this crappy circuit, you know? The Three Keatons went to England last year. Those folks hated the bit. *Ha-ted* it. Thought I was being abused," he said, and chuckled. "Can you imagine that?"

Yes. Absolutely. Without a doubt.

"So we came back to the States early," Buster continued. "Mr. Keith lost a bundle on us. He put us on the small-small-time circuit until we'd earned his losses back. And until the dust settled. Those newspapers over there really tore our act apart."

It didn't surprise me one bit that Mr. Keith—Whitting's boss, the one who owned most of the vaudeville circuits in the

U.S.—did this to the Keatons. I was actually a little surprised that he simply didn't ask for reimbursement in the form of Buster's indentured servitude. And from what I'd seen of Joe Keaton, he would've paid it.

Buster flipped through the pages more rapidly—*zip, zip, zip.* "You should see the big-time circuit, Hope. It's something else."

He raised his wistful eyes to mine. "You know I've played the Palace?"

"Really?" I asked. The Palace in New York City? Now that *was* something. I was no fan of vaudeville, but the *Palace*? I'd love to have seen it.

"Yeah . . . ," he said. "Holds two thousand people, you know. And there's a program in every single seat. Seats—not benches. Plush velvet seats. And ushers in fancy uniforms, and dressing rooms with private baths, and—"

Buster twisted the dime novel into tight tube and jammed it into the back pocket of his trousers. "Sorry," he mumbled. "I just—I really want to be done with this crappy tour now that we're back in Chicago."

Huh. How about that? Buster Keaton and I had something in common.

That evening, after I recounted and stashed in my trunk the $37.25 I'd made so far, I prepared for bed. I cursed the pipes in the community bathroom. They shook and screamed at me as if I were torturing them. A trickle of brown water plipped from the faucet. Huck. No way was I washing up with that swill.

I gathered my washcloth and powder to depart the tiny

bathroom when Myra Keaton entered. I lowered my gaze, hoping that a lack of eye contact would discourage any interaction. I was mistaken.

"You," she said by way of a greeting. I paused.

"I got something for you." She reached into the pocket of her flashy purple dress. What could Myra Keaton possibly give me? A poisoned apple, perhaps? I half expected a witchy cackle to follow.

"I've been holding on to these until I ran into you," she said. A mishmash of newspaper articles fanned in her hand. She pulled one from the middle of the stack and held it up for me to see.

"Look here. One fellow in Canada is selling umbrellas that are supposed to have this special kind of lead in them that protects you from Halley's Comet. And, oh! Look at this one!" She pulled another article from her collection. "This guy is actually selling trips to the moon to escape the comet. Trips to the moon!" She threw her head back and laughed so loud it echoed off the tiled walls of the bathroom.

She snapped back to attention and gripped my upper arm. Myra Keaton leaned in close, and I could smell the layer of sweat that lingered beneath her powder and perfume.

"But your idea is the best one of all, sugar," she whispered. "Low overhead, almost believable. Wish I'd thought of it myself."

She winked at me, thrust the newspaper articles into my hand, pivoted on her high heel, and sashayed out the door.

My stilled heart leapt back to life. That woman would be the end of me, for certain. Why else would she collect all these articles, if she weren't trying to get a piece of my profits? Suddenly all the money I'd worked for seemed in jeopardy.

If Nick and I were to be unemployed in ten days, I would have to swallow my fears from earlier today and get back to work tomorrow.

May 11, 1910

Seven Days
till the End of the World.

NEWS HEADLINE

Earth Ready to Enter Tail of the Comet

I hesitated before ducking through the shaft of light that transported me into the murky alley between Heel Thy Sole and the Orpheum Palace Theatre. The points at which the rusty knife had pierced the skin on my neck tingled. Could I do it? Could I go back there again?

The clouds covering the sun shifted, and as they did, I caught a glimpse of something familiar lingering in the darkness: the flash of jewelry, piles of it, hanging around the neck of the lady with the gleaming white teeth. Next to her stood the man leaning on his glorious carved skull-and-crossbones cane. The rustle of beads in hair, the mewing of the redhead's tiny baby . . .

Yes, I could do it. I had to. I plunged in.

And can I add? It didn't hurt to have Buster's hand on the small of my back, either.

"Good morning, folks!" I chirped. It sounded false, but hey, I was *there*.

Business was swift that morning, and several newcomers were in attendance. I kept keen eyes on them, flinching every time they reached in their pockets, only to withdraw another shiny quarter.

Two of the newcomers were Asian, speaking perhaps Chinese. Their soft, whispery syllables belied the harsh hacking of my German Coins, a couple of regulars. Added to the mix that morning was a lilting Irish brogue and a honkish New Englander. It was a lovely symphony of phonics, and it calmed me.

A new Coin with tiny spectacles and a large, twitching mustache strode forward. He traded a pill for a quarter, but then paused and peered at me over his glasses. He pinched the mint between his thumb and forefinger.

"These protect against cyanogen gas, yes?"

It shook me from my lulled state. "Pardon?"

"Cyanogen gas! If it does not protect against cyanogen gas, then I must insist upon a refund!"

Buster leaned around me. "Most certainly, sir. These pills—"

"Because there is no doubt that the comet's tail contains cyanogen gas!" the man bellowed. His face turned red and his forehead grew bumpy with worry. He whipped toward the rest of my customers.

"Cyanogen gas is found in prussic acid, a poison so powerful that a single drop on the tongue would cause *instant* death." As he said *instant,* he snapped his fingers, as though underscoring how quickly our deaths would occur. Instant.

He then appeared to crumple like a wadded-up sheet of paper. "The spectrum shows very plainly that this gas is present in the tail of the comet," he said, wilting. He pushed his spectacles up his nose with his thumb.

"I need to know if these will protect me," he whispered. His eyes were black, like a candle that had been snuffed out the instant he'd said *instant*.

I couldn't lie to this man. I didn't want to. There was a comet flinging toward us at this very minute, now as big around as the head of a spool of thread when viewed in the nighttime sky.

It's easy to be a hero from a safe distance.

"I'm helping the only way I know how," I said. I filled my lungs with air and offered my hand to him in handshake. "I'm Hope."

He stood and straightened his bow tie, as if thinking he'd made a fool of himself before this group of strangers. "Indeed," he said. He shook my hand with a soft, warm grip, and left.

Buster rolled his eyes at me, trying to make light. "Cyanogen gas?" he whispered.

But the exchange had pricked a hole in my veneer. *Could it be true?* I rolled my eyes back at Buster, hoping he couldn't see my doubt.

I made a vow to myself, then, that I would do more to prepare. For this comet. For our unemployment. I had to raise more money. I couldn't be caught unawares. Not ever again.

I reached into my pocket and stroked the square of red flannel there.

I am so, so sorry, Mama.

Nick and I stood behind the curtains, awaiting our next performance. I peered out onto the stage, watching our lead-in act: Dr. Electricity. Nick listened intently as well, and even scribbled notes on a crumpled program. He was still biting on Dr. Electricity's bit, still countering Dr. E's "science" with his more naturalistic point of view. But it was working; Nick and I had received a standing ovation at every performance for the last three days. I'd never seen Nick so light in his shoes.

Or Dr. Electricity so jumpy. Dr. E was already a jittery little man, but Nick's tactics seemed to make the fellow more cautious than ever.

> ***Cautious? Dr. E is so cautious, he wears a belt and suspenders at the same time!***

Dr. Electricity's awful wardrobe was comprised mainly of pants with too-big, cinched waists and shirts with too-tiny, pinched neckholes. His big head sprung forth from his collar like a balloon on a stick. He snuffled and mumbled throughout much of the act, but he still managed to generate much excitement about the newest and greatest electrical contraptions. His lectures on *stuff*—electric lightbulbs and phonographs and kinetoscopes—were amazing. Even though Nick thought these things were little more than flashy junk, I thought them the daisy.

Today Dr. Electricity entertained his audience by touching a luminescent glass globe, which made the fluff of hair atop his head stand at attention. Hands off the globe, the hair would fall. Hands on, the hair was erect. The audience roared.

But Dr. Electricity hushed them by saying, "It's so fragile, isn't it? This orb. Like our Mother Earth, awaiting her fate as Mr. Halley's Loyal Visitor calls upon us." He had taken the directive set forth by Whitting, to include Halley's Comet within our acts. I leaned in for a better view of his speech.

"But to calm our fears, to aid our anxieties, it is best to remember that man is *part* of the universe," he continued. "He is composed of exactly the same chemicals which form the stars, the earth, the oceans, and space." Although difficult to see from my vantage point, I imagined that the audience did not care for this train of thought. Man and stars alike?

"Remember that you are composed of *exactly the same materials* which make the comet. You are its kin! The same *stupendous cause* which put you into orbit, flung that comet into space!" Dr. Electricity was obviously passionate about this idea, as he kept jabbing his thumb at the audience in a strange pointing motion.

You could've heard a tear drop in that theater, it was so quiet. It was apparent that the crowd did not take kindly to being broken down into chemicals and materials and elements.

Elements. I thought of cyanogen gas and felt as if my throat were sealing shut from thick, poisonous gas at that exact moment.

Nick had stopped jotting down notes. "Well, now, *he* bombed, didn't he?" he whispered over my shoulder. He crunched down on a Sen-Sen mint. I could hear the smile in his voice.

Dr. Electricity swallowed, regained his composure, and placed his hands on the orb one last time. His hair shot up, the audience forgot about its fragile composition, and they giggled like a group of schoolchildren.

Dr. Electricity shuffled past me, desperate to get off that stage. I grabbed his elbow.

"Excuse me, Dr. Electricity? Do you think we should fear Halley's Comet?"

He paused, looking at me as if he'd never seen me before. "The newspapers tell us that the world's greatest scientists say no," he said.

I released the breath I didn't realize I'd been holding.

Then he looked at Nick, and his eyes narrowed. His eyes darted back to mine. It was apparent he finally realized who I was: the magician's assistant.

His impish face twisted into a cruel grin, his hatred for Nick apparent. "But one mustn't believe everything she reads, girlie."

He pushed his cart and his fragile glass orb away.

Nick and I performed a relatively simple ring trick that day, juggling and entangling and intertwining eight large, silver hoops. The hardest part of this bit was making sure the hoops didn't get snarled together. When done flawlessly, the trick was graceful, poetic, like planets in orbit.

Nick compared the intertwining of hoops to the intertwining

of our fates, the strength of the chain of hoops to the strength of our souls united against the comet.

"We are not mere *elements*," he bellowed, once again countering Dr. Electricity's argument. "We are *elemental*! Earth, water, air, fire—all of us, each one!

"If I may, allow me to paraphrase sir Walt Whitman. . . ."

Oh, huck, I thought. *Here's where we'll lose them.*

Nick continued,

The comet shall not long possess the sky.
It devours the stars only in apparition.
Jupiter shall emerge, be patient, watch again
another night . . .
They are immortal, all those stars both silvery
and golden shall shine out again,
The great stars and the little ones shall shine out
again, they endure,
The vast immortal suns and the long-enduring
pensive moons shall shine again.

To my never-ending surprise, we received yet another standing ovation. Nick shined like the immortal sun as we dashed offstage.

Ever hear the one about the performer who
was so full of himself, he turned inside out?

Whitting awaited us. He chawed on an unlit cigar, a lump of gummy tobacco stuck between his front teeth.

"Moving you on the bill, Nick," he grunted. He pointed at my father with the end of his cigar. "Need you in slot five. Starting next show, you hear?"

He grunted and wobbled off. Huck. The other performers were going to *loathe* us, now that we'd caused a shuffle in the schedule in the middle of the day. There had been a bump in the schedule just yesterday, when Whitting punished Bert Savoy for the automobile shenanigans by placing him after the Cherry Sisters. Huck! What a nightmare.

But Nick's eyes glowed. He placed one hand on each of my shoulders. "Five, Hopeful! Did you hear that? Slot five! That spot is for acts on the move! We must be on our way up!" He practically skipped out a side door.

On the move, I thought. It was true. Slot five was for acts stuck in performance limbo, acts that the management just didn't know how to categorize. But "on the move" didn't necessarily mean we were moving up. It might mean we were moving *out.*

Which was it? Could it really be *out*? I smiled. It could.

I could be *out.*

May 12, 1910

SIX DAYS

till the End of the World.

NEWS HEADLINE

Hey! Look Out! The Comet's Tail Is Coming Fast!

Though we'd only done so four times, Nick adored performing in slot five. It was the last "real" act before intermission, so Nick fancied that we were now a mini grande finale. Today, we performed a quick-change trick, in which we changed our clothing rapidly behind fluttering sheets and flapping flags. It sounds quite dull, I know, but the audience thought it astounding. (Ah, if only they knew how versatile sixteen outfits loosely bound with shoestrings can be.) The crowd rewarded our efforts, complete with Nick's lecture on how "we can change our ways to change the course of the comet," with yet another standing ovation.

We hustled offstage left, to rousing applause. I squeezed between two bicycles and a unicycle lined up at the curtain's edge. And though I had just, in effect, changed my clothes before hundreds of strangers, I ducked into the dressing room to change back into my street outfit.

And by "dressing room," I mean a rotting, dusty curtain tacked into a dark corner backstage. There was no light in this nook, and changing without sticking out some random bare body part was next to impossible. Most performers ignored this dressing room altogether, preferring instead to change their clothes before God and everyone backstage. This was, of course, not an option for me.

Modest? I'm not modest. I merely prefer to bathe in all my clothes.

The act following ours was a dumb act and signaled the beginning of intermission. *Dumb* meant it was an act in which no one sang or spoke, not *dumb* as in *stupid*. Though I suppose it depended on whom you asked, which category Boris Frolov and his family of cyclists fell under.

The Frolovs hopped upon their bikes and wheeled onstage. That was usually the last I saw of their act; their backsides heading into the spotlight. But today, after I emerged from the dressing nook, there was quite a commotion in the house. I peeked around the curtain to see what was going on with the audience.

The Frolovs were fine; Boris, the father, balanced on a unicycle while his youngest son stood atop his shoulders. Two more Frolovs—named Ivan and Lena, I'd learned through a conversation of pointing and naming—pedaled bicycles in circles around them. They kicked the front wheel of their bikes up every so often so that they, too, rode on one wheel. It was a crowded stage, and I worried a little for them but reminded myself that these folks did this four times a day.

Then I saw the trouble: a burly, bearded man in the front row. "Get those Russkies off the stage!" he growled. He was massive, taking up the same amount of space on his bench as the three people next to him. His salt-and-pepper hair was oily and hung in clumps. I hadn't noticed him during our act, but then I couldn't have—in our act, the house lights were darkened, but as this was intermission, the house lights were raised.

"Damn worthless Russians should ride their bikes back to their own country!" he shouted. Ah, yes, and he was a genius as well. He spat tiny chunks of peanut as he shouted this. There were dozens of peanut shells lying about his dirty boots.

"Get 'em OUT!" the beast bellowed, and he chucked a handful of peanuts onstage at the cyclists.

It was as ugly a scene as you can possibly imagine: Ivan's back wheel bumped over a peanut, causing the bike to skid out from under him. Lena crashed into him from behind, and the youngest Frolov, atop his father's shoulders, toppled backward and landed on a twisted left arm.

The whole time? Not a single one of them ever stopped smiling. Ever.

The Frolovs picked themselves up, dusted themselves off, and took their bows before shuffling offstage, pushing their damaged bikes beside them.

"Are you okay?" I asked the youngest Frolov as he walked by rubbing his arm.

"Okay, okay!" father Boris said in a thick accent. His eyes shot to a nearby corner, and mine followed. Whitting stood there, scratching his chin, watching the Frolovs over the bump in his beak.

"Is okay!" Boris nodded too emphatically. He pushed the littlest Frolov toward the exit. "Is okay. Be ready for next show, yes!"

Lena walked by me and nodded. "Next show." She gave me the thumbs-up sign I'd taught her once on the train.

They tumbled outdoors, garbling Russian to one another. The tiny Frolov boy locked eyes with me briefly before he was shuffled away.

Whitting cracked his knuckles, apparently satisfied that he wouldn't have to fire the stumbling Frolov family then and there. He folded himself through a wall of curtain, heading to stage right.

A wave of heat washed over me. This circuit was a trap of fear and dread, fueled by intimidation and a lack of practical skills. Like so many vaudevillians, I couldn't type and I didn't know shorthand. My formal schooling was limited, and I doubted many employers would consider Nick's "brain fertilizer" substantial learning. At least I could read. But I was too small for most factory work. And Nick? Sheesh. But we'd find something out there, after we were fired. We had to. That's why so many vaudevillians toured until they dropped dead. They could not escape because there was nowhere else for them to go.

Nowhere else to go. That must be how my Coins viewed this approaching comet. With fear and dread, because there was simply nowhere else to go. I mean, how do you escape a *comet,* for heaven's sake?

You don't.

𝕿hat evening, the chatter among my customers was dead. The only sound was the jingle of quarters being exchanged for mints. Their mood was somber, their faces, stoic.

"What's the matter?" I asked Nathalia. I couldn't help but learn their names, listening to their conversations over the past handful of days. "You are usually so full of theories."

Nathalia shook her head, and the beads in her braids rustled like crunching dry leaves. "Girl, tomorrow is Friday the thirteenth," she whispered.

I had to bite my lip to keep from laughing. Fear of a comet—yes, I understood. But fear of Friday the 13th? And yet I had to consider my audience. People purchasing anti-comet pills would indeed be worried about such matters.

"We've survived many an end-of-week thirteen," I said, thrusting my chin up.

"Ah, but this one!" Calvin hitched his thumbs through the straps of his coveralls and bounced on his toes. He bent in half, leaning toward me. "The comet's to rise at two forty-seven a.m. tomorrow. Added together, that's thirteen again!"

"Double thirteen!" said Mr. Bruce. He tapped his carved cane. "Tell me *that's* not something to fear!"

I shook my head. As they did with the sun, astronomers made predictions as to when the comet would rise—break the horizon—each evening. These predictions were printed beside the sunrise estimates in our daily newspapers.

Double thirteen—pah! But I suddenly wished that I'd waited for Buster to finish his performance before I'd come back here to peddle pills.

Double thirteen. Rubbish.

Right?

May 13, 1910

FIVE DAYS

till the End of the World.

NEWS HEADLINE

Host of Converts at Revivals, All Afraid of Comet

A fine layer of dew still coated everything in the murky alley the next morning when Buster and I ducked between Heel Thy Sole and the Orpheum Theatre. Even in the dark alley, the sheen of dew trapped snatches of sunlight, and the garbage canisters and splintered wooden crates sparkled like they were strewn with gems. Only the fetid smell reminded me of the business at hand.

"Morning, folks!" Buster sang to the customers already waiting in long queues. "Is this a gorgeous morning or what?" He winked at me, and my stomach flipped like Chekhov's acrobatic dog. I told myself it was *not* the wink, but instead the indistinguishable breakfast gravy I'd devoured that morning.

This morning's gravy was so thick, when I stirred it, the room spun around!

My Coins shuffled and murmured, not at all appreciative of the delicate light show the universe was bestowing upon us this morning.

"What's the matter?" I asked, pulling the pills from my pocket. They pinged in the metal tin, and I noticed the calm that washed over my Coins as they did. "We survived the comet rising upon Double Thirteen, did we not?" I neglected to add that I had lain awake most of last evening, only falling asleep once we had passed well into the three o'clock hour.

"We did, we did," Calvin said. His eyes were red rimmed, like they carried the weight of his worry. I glanced at the rest of my customers: puffy, black circles under their eyes, droopy postures, gray pallor. The picture of sleepless concern. Among us, only Buster was pink and smiling.

"It's just so worrisome," Nathalia whispered. She shifted, and her large knitting bag slooped off her shoulder. The beads in her hair tinkled softly. "This comet—I think about it every moment of every day. I might just needle myself to death before she even draws near!"

Mr. Bruce nodded and leaned too heavily on his cane. I feared it might slide out from under his weight in this greasy alley. "I'm considering emptying my bank account and donating it all to my church."

I awoke as if someone had snapped the elastic in my wristband. "No!" I shouted, much too loudly for this narrow space.

I shook my head. "You cannot do it. You cannot live without some savings!"

My voice sounded wavery and thin, as if I were hearing it through one of Dr. Electricity's phonographs. Buster studied me for a moment, then the corners of his mouth turned up ever so slightly.

"What the kid here means is, if you're scared, then you should buy some more anti-comet pills!" He swooshed his hand at the tin of mints in a grand gesture. Always a performer, that one.

"No." I shook my head in a rapid twitch. "No, that's not what I mean at all." I glared at Buster but softened my gaze once I realized he was only trying to help me.

I felt panic swell in my chest as I imagined the danger these people would be in if they had no savings. I knew firsthand what that kind poverty felt like. It was the darkest of night, like the inky black nothingness between stars. It is next to impossible to escape darkness that complete unscathed. We—Nick and my mother and I—didn't.

I swore I would never experience that again. I didn't want my customers to experience it, either. Before, I'd not allowed myself to consider the financial circumstances of my Coins. It would make it too difficult to sell them mints disguised as pills. But *knowing* they'd be broke was something entirely different.

I swallowed several gulps of air and approached the gentleman leaning on his carved cane. I laid a gentle hand on his humped back. "No, listen, Mr. Bruce. It's a noble idea, donating everything you have to your church. But you're going to survive this comet. I'm going to help you. I promise. And when you do, you're going to want a stash of money set aside."

"Yeah, 'cause who knows what our world is going to look like on May nineteenth?" Buster said behind me. I looked over my shoulder, expecting him to wear a smirk or some other sassy expression. But he was totally forthcoming; I could tell he meant what he said. I smiled at him, despite the dire topic of conversation. I smiled because Buster had a tiny speck of doubt, as did I. I smiled because Buster was starting to care for these Coins, too.

Mr. Bruce nodded, weary but satiated for one more day. He dug in the pocket of his trousers for a quarter.

"No money today, folks," I said, straightening. *Had I really said that? Indeed, it* was *my voice!*

I cleared my throat to rid it of my own lingering objections. "The anti-comet pills are on me today." *Breathe, Hope. You can do this.* "In fact, if any of you are having trouble paying for your medicine," I shook the tin of mints at the crowd, "let me know and we'll work something out."

I felt briefly noble, like a brilliant comet streaking across a night sky, before it destroyed everything with its ephemeral wake.

After my final performance of the day, I dashed to change clothes and make one final round in the alley before falling into bed for the evening. As I was ducking out the Negro door at the rear of the theater, a hand gripped my elbow. Tightly.

I turned and leaned immediately back, as I realized I was

136

standing face-to-face with Joe Whitting. *How short he is,* was my first thought, *that he's the same size as a petite thirteen-year-old girl!*

Then: *Huck. How can a human being smell like that and not be dead?*

"Come with me," he grumbled around his gummy cigar. Whitting never lit his cigars, just chawed them until they fell apart in his mouth. He spat the remnants wherever he was, no exceptions. I imagined he had a mass of brown goo about his bedchamber. The thought made me shudder. That'd take care of those boardinghouse ants!

He pulled me into a room with a sign on the door that read, OFFICE. I'd seen the door before, of course, but hadn't paid it much mind. The inner workings of the Orpheum Palace Theatre were not high on my list of ponderances.

He closed the door behind him and shoved me toward a wooden chair in the middle of the room. "Sit," he said. My mind finally registered this flurry of events and my muscles clenched. Witting circled behind a teetering desk piled with paper and sat on a burgundy leather seat.

Whitting glared at me over the desk. I realized my knee was twitching and I crossed my legs at the ankles to stop it. Whitting glared some more. I switched my ankles to left over right. He glared more and spat on the floor, but I didn't dare lower my eyes to see where he'd spat, as I knew he'd take that as a sign of weakness.

"You've been making a lot of money lately," he said. His eyes narrowed.

I decided to play dumb. I twirled a lock of my dark hair

betwixt my fingers. "Right. Nick's—erm, my father's act has been well-received these past few days, hasn't it?"

Whitting switched his cigar from the right side of his mouth to the left side with a shift of his jaws. "No, *you*. You're selling something on the side. I want to know what."

My heart dropped to the points of my shoes. *Mrs. Keaton sold me out!*

That gal's mouth is so big, she can whisper in her own ear!

I swallowed. "Selling, sir?"

Whitting waved his hand about like he was shooing a fly. "Don't play me for a fool, girl. What are you peddling in that back alley?"

Do I lie? No, I decided, he already knew I was selling *something*. Did it really matter what?

"Anti-comet pills," I said at last. Whiting said nothing. Absolutely nothing.

I must admit, I was initially surprised by his lack of reaction—there was no laughing, no yelling, no clarifying what he'd heard with an "anti-*what*?" This man was truly jaded.

But why wouldn't he be? He booked *vaudeville* acts for a living, for heaven's sake! He'd seen everything. I once overheard Whitting tell a tale of an act in which a man swallowed kerosene mixed with water. The man then spat the liquids on fire *in order*—kerosene blasted the blaze, and water doused it.

Whitting had, according to rumor, seen women juggling frogs. Kids used as mops. Once when we were in Bloomington, a performer mailed himself to Whitting to try to get a booking. This man had seen it all.

So of course anti-comet pills wouldn't faze him. They were simply the next in a long, strange series of life events for him.

Whitting laced his fingers and cracked his knuckles. "Managers get a cut of whatever performers make. You know this?"

I nodded. No sense in pointing out that my pills had nothing to do with my being a performer.

"Fifty percent," he said. He removed his cigar and laid the slimy thing on top of a stack of paper.

"What?" I said, before I could censor myself. Numbers flew through my head. If I didn't pay, Whitting would likely fire Nick today. Based on the sixty-some-odd dollars I had in my grouch bag and stashed in my Herkert & Meisel trunk, we'd likely be okay for a couple of months, until we could both find jobs. So yes, I *could* refuse to pay and get us fired.

Except then what would my customers do? There was no way I could sell pills behind the theater if we were ousted— even I wasn't so brazen as to attempt that! If I left now, with five days of doubt looming before us, there's no telling what kinds of things my Coins might do. Sell off all their goods, donate all their money . . . even . . . suicide? I shuddered. No, I told them I'd help them survive this comet. I promised. I won't leave them now that I've promised. I know what that feels like, to be left behind after someone has promised you they'd stay. It's a million pinpricks to your heart.

"Fifty percent," Whitting repeated. "And I want back pay."

Back pay! He wanted fifty percent of everything I'd already made! My mind whirred: There was no way he could know how much money I'd saved to date, right? No way was I forking over half my savings. Thirty dollars! No, he'd get a third of that, tops. I couldn't risk losing my home now. It was so close I was practically planting bulbs in the front flower beds. No, I'd take my chances on Whitting finding out the truth.

My stomach squeezed like a fist. There was no telling what he'd do if he found out the truth. Talk about a grande finale.

Just when you're about to make ends meet,
somebody comes along and moves the ends.

May 14, 1910

Four Days
till the End of the World.

NEWS HEADLINE

Ready for the End of the World?

Onstage the next day, Nick was attempting a trick he'd never tried before. He called it the Ticking Clocks. He needn't remind me that the clock was ticking; it seemed as though I felt each second tick off with a deafening *click*!

I disliked trying out new tricks before an audience. New tricks were often clumsy and obvious, but Nick's sudden popularity had inspired him to brave uncharted territory. So I stood awkwardly nearby, my hands raised in a giant letter *L*, wearing a garish dress that I believe had been crafted of sandpaper, for all its comfort.

Nick whisked a shiny silver alarm clock from his breast pocket. The clock was the size of a giant grapefruit and was far too lumpy and large to have been in his pocket the entire time. The audience gasped when it materialized.

"Hear that?" Nick said, holding the clock aloft. A hush fell over the crowd, and sure enough, the *tick . . . tick . . . tick . . .* of the clock was audible.

"That sound?" Nick whispered. "That's us, the whole of Earth, ticking toward our destiny."

The crowd shifted uncomfortably. Destiny weighed heavily these days.

Nick then pulled a silk handkerchief from his pocket and quickly produced another ticking clock from beneath its folds.

"But this is the time for hope!" he yelled, holding the second clock aloft. He shot me a quick wink at the somewhat-mention of my name.

I have to admit, Nick looked like he was having the time of his life!

He twiddled his fingers across the table, behind his hat, over the top of my head, producing three more clocks, *tick, tick, tick.* It was impressive, this new trick.

He hushed the crowd once again, and the sound of five clocks was soon the only sound to be heard. At first, the ticks sounded random, merely unsynchronized noises, but slowly, they merged together in harmony. Or did we just think they had?

"One plea!" Nick said, swooping his hand over the pyramid of alarm clocks he'd constructed. "If we, like these clocks, can synchronize our thoughts, summon our collective powers, and offer forth a singular, focused plea, we can save ourselves from Mr. Halley's fiery beast!"

"This is a time for miracles!" he whispered. And one by one, he snapped his fingers across the clocks, and one by one, they disappeared. I smiled. This was one amazing trick!

"The great Walt Whitman says of miracles," Nick began. Oh, huck. He was on a roll. Did he really have to go and bring Whitman into this?

"The great Whitman says:

Why, who makes much of a miracle?
As to me, I know of nothing else but miracles . . .
To me, every hour of the light and dark is a
*   miracle,*
Every cubic inch of space a miracle,
Every square yard of the surface of the earth
*   is spread with the same.*

"Moving this comet is not impossible! Our collective will *can* change its path! Miracles happen *every* day! Every day!" he shouted, and bent forward in a low bow, sweeping his arms in an exaggerated arc. There, at his feet, the pyramid of ticking clocks reappeared, perfectly aligned.

We took five, then six bows to our standing ovation, and bounded offstage.

"Nick, that was some trick!" I said. "You didn't tell me you'd been practicing that!"

Nick clamped an arm about my shoulders. "You haven't exactly been easy to find these days, Hopeful."

I snuck my eyes sidewise, expecting to see him scowling at me. Instead, he wore a huge grin. He leaned toward me.

"I hear you've made a *friend*," Nick whispered. By the way he cocked his head, I could tell he meant Buster. I half expected to burst into flames, the way I burnt with embarrassment.

"A friend, yes. A friend." I nodded, and from the edge of my vision, I saw Whitting approaching us. While never a welcome sight, I was at least glad for the need to change the topic.

I'd not told Whitting that Nick knew nothing of the comet pills. As he approached, I prayed silently that Whitting wouldn't mention them. Huck. Being a shyster sure was hard work.

"Nice work, Nick." Whitting smacked his gummy cigar. "Gonna switch you guys in the lineup again. Think you can perform in front of the curtain?"

Performing in front of the curtain meant we'd be just before a big act, one that they'd set up behind the curtain while we were on.

"Absolutely!" Nick said. He took off his jacket and mopped his brow with his trick handkerchief. I could tell he was thinking, *No way we can perform in that tiny space,* but passing up an opportunity like this one would be a massive career misstep. Not that that would matter to *me,* of course, but to Nick . . .

"Good. Gonna place you in front of the Keatons," Whitting said. Before he slid away, he paused just before me. He didn't look at me or speak to me, but I got the message:

Bring the money today.

Nick saw none of this. "Hopeful!" he shouted. He picked me up and spun me around. I hadn't seen him this excited since, well, I couldn't ever remember seeing him this excited.

"Us—me and you—opening for the Three Keatons! That's a

big honor, Hopeful. A big honor indeed. I'm heading back to the boardinghouse to figure out which acts we can do out front. Sheesh! Opening for the Three Keatons . . ." Nick practically skipped away, popping a handful of mints.

It *was* a huge honor, opening for the Keatons. But had we really earned it, or was Whitting just thanking me for the windfall that was coming his way?

Tick . . . tick . . . tick . . .

Huck. Could I really hear those infernal clocks still ticking? Surely not. And yet, I could.

Tick . . . tick . . . tick . . .

In my dingy, windowless room at the boardinghouse, I sat on the floor and counted out quarters for Whitting. No way was he getting half. Sure, I had enough money now to support Nick and myself for several weeks, but who knew when we'd find jobs? No, I'd give him a small cut, but not half. There was no way he could know it wasn't enough. Right?

My fingers grew black from touching mounds of slick, dirty quarters. I tried wiping them clean on my skirts, but the stains remained.

I wished we had a window in this tiny cell. The comet drew ever nearer, and though it was daytime, one could sometimes see a flicker of light against a brilliant blue sky. Mr. Halley's comet was powerful enough to outshine the sun. How could we *not* be afraid?

Perhaps Nick was correct. Perhaps we could will this comet away, just by wishing it so. I squinched my eyes shut:

Go away, comet. Go away. Spare us, comet. Go away.

My eyes shot open, and I quickly scanned my bedchamber to make certain no one had seen me participating in such a silly endeavor. Wishing away a comet! Pah!

I resumed my quarter counting, pausing to swipe my black-tainted fingers on my skirts. The blasted stains remained.

My fingers were still black from the hour I'd spent counting out quarters for Whitting. I hadn't had time to clean them before I brought the money to his office.

I dumped the hefty pouch on his desk, and it landed with a clinky *thud*.

Whitting grinned with half his face. "How much is it?" he asked, jutting his chin at the bag.

"Fifteen twenty-five, " I said. Approximately one-quarter of my comet pill earnings to date.

"Unh," he grunted in response.

I took a shaky breath. Did he know it wasn't the half he'd demanded?

Whitting lifted the sack of coins and dropped them into a desk drawer. Then he grunted again. I took that as my dismissal and left his office.

I was rubbing my hands together, trying to lessen the black stains on my fingertips, and bumped into Buster.

"Hey, kid!" he said, and smiled. A girl could get used to that smile, for certain.

He looked over my shoulder at the office door. "Everything okay?"

I didn't want to tell Buster that his mother had sold me out and that our hard-earned quarters were now lining Whitting's pockets. Well, his desk drawer, actually. I thought Buster would be disappointed in me if he learned I'd been caught. No, it was best to keep mum.

"Fine. Just uh . . ." I turned to the door, then back to Buster. "Nick and I have been moved on the bill. You are now looking at your opening act." I took a grand, sweeping bow.

Buster's grin grew, and my knees turned to jelly. "Hey, no kidding! That's swell!"

He grabbed my elbow and ushered me toward the side exit of the theater. "I've been looking for you, kid. C'mere."

"Looking for me?" I said it before I could censor myself. Drat! Why couldn't I at least *pretend* that handsome fellows looked for me on a regular basis?

These days, I was accustomed to leaving the theater through the rear exit, into the dark back alley and was surprised by the blast of sunlight and cool, crisp air that greeted us from the side door. Buster stopped short and dug in the pocket of his trousers.

"Here," he said, and thrust a folded note card my way. I unfolded the well-creased paper and read the scrolly message engraved inside:

MONSIEUR AND MADAME KEITH
REQUEST THE HONOUR OF YOUR PRESENCE
ON THE NIGHT OF MAY 17
TO MARK THE IMMINENT PASSAGE OF EARTH
THROUGH THE TAIL OF HALLEY'S COMET.

"Wow," I said with a chuckle. "So I'm not the only one who's noticed there's a comet streaking toward us." I held the invitation out to Buster, but he didn't take it.

He rubbed the outer seam of his trousers, like I'd seen him do in his poker game. "No, uh, I'm going to that," he said. He pointed to the invitation. "My parents are, too. Mr. Keith is hosting it. You know—Benjamin Keith?"

Did I know Benjamin Keith? He was only Mr. Whitting's boss, the owner of our vaudeville circuit, the owner of almost every vaudeville circuit in the country. As wealthy and as cutthroat as they come, I'd heard.

"You know Benjamin Keith?" I asked. I stood there, still awkwardly holding the invitation out to Buster, and he still didn't take it.

"Yes. No. Well, kind of. My parents know him. I wanted to see . . ." He rubbed the seam of his trousers harder. If I didn't know better, I'd say Buster Keaton was nervous.

"You want to go, too? You know, as a friend? Of mine?"

I think my throat must've locked up on me, because all I could do was nod. "Sure," I finally managed to say. "I mean, yes. Yes, thank you."

Buster nodded, too, then smiled. "Great. Good. I'm glad you can make it. You'll know a few others there besides me. My dad and mom. And Mr. Whitting'll probably be there, too." He walked past me, toward the boardinghouse.

Me. At a party. With Myra Keaton and Joe Whitting.

Oh, huck. My knees knocked together from nerves, I was sure of it. Should I go? Would Nick even let me go?

My black-tainted fingers still held the worn invite.

This would be interesting.

That evening, I was sick-nervous to tell Cross-Eyed Jane that Buster had invited me to a party at the Palmer House Hotel. When I finally choked it out, she squealed like a child at Christmas, picked me up in a giant hug, and twirled me around before I demanded she put me down.

"She's a high society gal now, ain't she?" Jane said with a wink. At the ceiling.

I laughed and climbed onto my cot, careful not to dip my toes in acid. "I doubt that."

Jane bounced on the edge of her bed, her piles of fake jewelry clanging. "Oh! What's she gonna wear?" She strode over to my trunk and flipped it open before I could stop her.

"Jane, wait!" I said, and hopped off the bed.

There, atop everything else in my trunk, was a massive pile of quarters. It looked like a pirate's booty, this trunk splayed open with mounds of sparkling coins heaped inside. I hadn't yet hidden them again from when I'd counted out Whitting's share earlier.

Jane's wrinkled lips let out a long, low whistle. "She's sitting pretty, for sure, ain't she?" Jane turned to me, and instead of the pride I thought I'd see in her eyes, I saw fear.

I was confused. "Jane, are you sure you don't want a cut of this?"

"Naw, girl! No!" she whispered. She pulled a grouch bag from beneath a slidy pile of coins and began shoveling them into the bag. "She just . . . oh, my! A girl's gotta be careful with all this, hear?"

Jane shoveled piles of quarters into bags as quickly as I'd ever seen her move. Finally, she looked up at me with her one good eye.

"She's gotta stow this somewhere, understand? Cash like this ain't safe here. This here makes her a sitting duck."

The tone of her warning scared me. I nodded and helped her scoop coins into bags. At last we had them somewhat concealed beneath a crocheted scarf.

We sat, winded, on the nasty floor of our room, side by side. Moving that much money that fast was hard work. Finally, Jane grinned and slapped my knee.

"And here I was, worried about what she should wear. Lovey can just go buy herself a new Butterick's pattern!"

I narrowed my eyes at her in a kidding sort of way. "I'm not wasting twenty cents on a new dress pattern. Not for some stupid Benjamin Keith! I'll just wear something . . . of my own?" I knew as I said it, I had nothing appropriate. My clothes weren't exactly the peak of high fashion.

I've worn one dress so long, it's been back in style three times!

Jane threw her head back in a giant cackle. She hoisted herself off the floor with a massive grunt. "Naw, she won't. This event is special! We'll just dig around in the costume trunk, girlie. I ain't been to a soiree yet that couldn't be attended in a spiffy vaudeville getup!"

Ah, yes. And wasn't that poetic? Me, going to my first ball, in a costume.

Still just playing the part.

May 15, 1910

THREE DAYS
till the End of the World.

NEWS HEADLINE

Changes Reported in Comet

I snuck down the single flight of crusty stairs and crept toward Nick's room, trying to keep my jingling to a minimum. I transported almost fifty dollars, mostly in quarters, in the uplifted folds of my skirt. It was as heavy as toting a bucket of wet sand.

My aim was to hide the money in Nick's trunk. Nick wasn't known for his powers of observation. I'd stashed items there before, when I knew my trunk would be over the weight limit, and he'd paid them no mind. Of course, those things had been a box of stolen cookies and a hairbrush I'd pinched from a boardinghouse in Iowa City. I was hoping he wouldn't delve to the depths of his trunk before we were fired.

Nick was at the theater, trying to figure out how on earth we'd be able to perform in such a tiny space as to allow us to open for the Three Keatons. He'd be gone for hours.

I'd expected his room to be unlocked—Nick was not one to remember such a logical action as locking his boardinghouse door. But alas, he'd managed to do so today—drat! I plucked a hairpin from my hair and made quick work of the brass pin tumbler lock while the heaping sack of quarters sagged in the folds of my skirts. Picking locks was another thing one masters as a magician's assistant.

Nick did not have a roommate. Let's just say that by now, most of our fellow performers knew that boarding with Nick meant discussions into the wee hours of the morning about such fascinating topics as predestination and prohibition, neither topics of interest to our troupe mates.

Nick's room was orderly to the point of being sparse. One candle, a box of matches, and three books sat on his bedside table. I emptied the contents of my skirt onto his cot, and the sack of quarters rolled forth like a fat, dead hen. A hen made of clinky metal.

His Herkert & Meisel trunk rested at the foot of his bed, and it, thankfully, was unlocked. I kicked open its lid with the toe of my boot, as if touching it with my shoe was somehow less of an infraction than touching it with my fingertips. My black-stained fingertips. They bore black smudges all the time now, from the number of coins I touched on a daily basis.

The contents inside Nick's trunk were just as orderly as the rest of his room: a clean comb, several additional books, three tins of Sen-Sen mints, a few small props, and a crisp *Chicago Daily Tribune*. It might be more difficult to hide a sack of money in here than I'd imagined.

I hefted the bag of quarters and dropped it with a *clunk* to the bottom of the trunk. I covered the mound of money with a quilt of Nick's, but it was apparent something lurked beneath the blanket. I tried unfolding the newspaper and laying it across the obvious addition, and noticed that a column sporting the headline CHANGES REPORTED IN THE COMET was marked with Nick's handwriting.

The article read: ". . . it was announced at Harvard Observatory that the tail of the celestial visitor is lengthening and spreading in a fan shape, which ensures that the Earth will pass through the tail about 5 million miles from its extreme end."

Nick had underlined "lengthening and spreading," and noted, "Our collective will is working! The gasses are dissipating, their powers weakening!"

An arrow underlined and shot forth from the words, "5 million miles," to a place where Nick had scrawled: "Man is so vain! He flatters himself that he has succeeded in understanding the delicate intricacies of the universe through science. But Mother Nature can and does call forth the comets and whatever other wonderful and alarming agencies she pleases."

I turned the paper clockwise, then counter to read Nick's handwriting. He was obviously making notes to use onstage. Beneath the article was an illustration that the *Tribune* had included to demonstrate the power of this ferocious comet:

A drawing of a comet, coupled with: "Halley's Comet travels 139,920 feet/second."

A drawing of a gun, coupled with: "Bullet from 13-inch gun travels 2,950 feet/second"

A drawing of a bi-level aeroplane, coupled with: "Aeroplane travels about 99 feet/second"

A drawing of a train, coupled with: "20th Century Limited at its fastest travels about 85 feet/second"

Below these, Nick had sketched a person smelling a flower, with the words, "Appreciation of nature: 0 feet/second"

I couldn't help but grin.

Then, a small notation in the corner of the newspaper caught my eye. It was tiny and scrawled in an obvious state of hurry or disarray:

"I miss you M."

M. Mary.

My mother. He missed her. He did.

I blinked back the tears that threatened to spill out on his paper and smudge the only proof I had that my father actually remembered my mother. That she had once walked this earth, had once been his wife.

I always sort of suspected that he was happy that she was no longer here, keeping us tied down to a normal house and a normal life. That with her gone, he was free to tramp about the country.

But he *missed* her?

My father. He'd gain twenty pounds if he swallowed his pride.

I ripped off the corner of the paper that carried Nick's admission and tucked it into the red square of flannel in my pocket. Nick missed my mother. . . .

But I had no time to ponder this. A key in the door and a mumbling just beyond interrupted me. *Nick!* I tossed the newspaper atop my stack of coins and slammed the lid of the trunk.

The door flew open, and for the second time in a matter of moments, I had to blink in order to make sense of what my eyes saw.

Whitting?

He stopped short when he saw me, and his jowls jiggled as he did so. The ring of keys hooked on his finger swayed. I recalled, then, his warning to us on our first day in Chicago: "Rumor on the circuit is that this boardinghouse of ours is a real black hole, as in things you bring in sometimes don't make it out. Hide your stash."

It was now apparent that the fault did not lie with our house manager, or even a string of crooked house managers strewn across the nation, as we had been told.

"You," he spat. He stepped inside and kicked the door shut with his heel.

My throat swelled with panic. There were no windows in this room. The only escape was blocked by Whitting's stumpy body.

"What're you doing in here?" he asked. His eyes narrowed to tiny black slits.

My fear turned to anger, and I felt as if I were a match being dragged across the striking strip, just prior to bursting into flame.

"I could ask you the same thing," I said. Oh, huck. Had I really said that?

A guttural growl came from Whitting, and he shuffled across the room and knotted a fistful of my dress fabric near my neck. He was surprisingly strong for such an overweight elf.

"You—on the male floor? Give me one reason why I shouldn't fire you right now!" As he yelled this, a few strands of his oiled hair slipped from its duty in covering his bald head and fell over his forehead in clumps.

Do it! I wanted to shout. *Fire us!* Oh, I was so close.

But I couldn't leave. Not until after the comet had passed. I'd promised my Coins.

I swallowed past the lump in my throat. "Besides the fact that Nick and I are now your second-biggest act, you mean?"

Whitting twisted his wrist and tightened his grip on my dress. The fabric burned raw against my skin like a rope.

"Easy," I whispered, hoping to douse the blackness in his eyes. "You can't fire me. Not yet. Not until the comet has passed. Think of all the money you'd lose."

Whitting's grip loosened slightly, and I twisted my neck to ease the pain.

"You can't sell those people my pills," I continued. "They'd see right through you. No, you need me to peddle pills right up until May eighteenth. If you want to fire me then, so be it."

Whitting turned me loose and pushed me toward Nick's door in one motion. "Go, then," he grumbled. "Don't ever let me see you on the male floor again."

I opened the door, but paused before I left.

"Aren't you coming?" I asked. I held an open palm to the door.

157

Whitting now had a choice to make. Stay, and give me the proof I needed that he was our thief (as if I really needed proof!), or go, and miss out on any goodies that might be lying about in Nick's room (including my newly stashed coin collection). I could see him calculating the risks in his head: Would the other performers believe the magician's assistant when she told them Whitting was the one ransacking our rooms? Or should he stay and pilfer to his heart's content?

Oh, merciful heavens. *Please let him follow me!* I didn't dare look at the trunk, for fear that my face would give away its contents.

I watched Whitting's eyes flit over Nick's candle, his matches, his books. He shrugged, as if he didn't care about these pitiful little items. But I could tell he understood that we were now even—he knew I was a shyster, and I knew he was a thief.

"Let's go," he grumbled, crossing to the door. He slicked his greasy hair back into place atop his head. "It appears as though everything's in order here. Good thing I do these spot checks. Keeps the stealing by the housekeepers to a minimum."

Mmm-hmm. Yes. Spot checks.

I wouldn't believe Joe Whitting if he said he was lying!

Later that day, Buster and I doled out pills behind the Orpheum Theatre. I debated whether to tell him everything—that Whitting was a thief and a blackmailer, that his mother could indeed *not* be trusted, when Buster shook an almost-empty tin of mints before me, waking me from my swirling thoughts.

"Ho-*ope!*" he said in a way that made me realize he'd been saying my name for quite some time. "Are these the last of the pills?"

The candies tinged about inside the tin. I flipped open the metal box and saw three flour-coated mints. Did I have more?

"That's it," I said, shaking my head. How could I have done something so stupid as to run out of pills?

Sometimes I'm so absentminded! I once cut my finger and forgot to bleed!

"I'll need to, um, get some more," I said.

As I said this, my Coins shifted and murmured like they'd been told that no more food was available, ever.

"Wha—when do you think you might have more?" Nathalia asked. The beads in her hair trembled.

"Should we wait here for you?" said Mr. Bruce. "We should, shouldn't we? We'll just wait right here. . . ." He propped his cane against the brick wall of the theater and leaned next to it, like he was preparing for a long stay.

"Folks, folks!" Buster said. He raised his arms over his head and patted the air, palms down, in a giant calming gesture. "The kid and I will run and grab some more pills from—er, the shaman." He glanced at me out of the corner of his eye, and

I saw a devilish gleam there. Had I not known him better, I wouldn't have seen it at all.

"We'll be back this evening, folks," he said. He took me by the elbow (*zing!*), and steered me out of the rising panic. "Come back this evening."

"Late!" I called over my shoulder, calculating the amount of time it would take to transform all those mints into pills.

Buster turned loose of my elbow once we were free of the alley (fizzle . . .), and we walked two blocks up to a trolley car stop.

The green-and-red trolley clanged and dinged to a stop before us just a moment later, and we climbed aboard. The twenty-some-odd seats were full, and Buster and I stood in the rear of the car, gripping the leather loops that dangled from the ceiling. Every once in a while, the trolley would jerk to a stop, and my back would be thrown into Buster's chest. I hoped it would happen more often.

I felt Buster lean over my shoulder to whisper something to me, and every hair on my neck and arm stood at attention. I realized that, stupidly, I hadn't heard a word he said. Sheesh.

"I'm sorry," I said, twisting around while still holding on to the leather loop. "I didn't hear what you—"

CRASH! CRASH! CRASH!

Before I could figure out where the deafening explosions were coming from, Buster tackled me and we fell to the floor of the trolley. Shards of glass rained down on top of us and tinkled about the trolley as though they were magical instead of deadly.

"It's the comet!" a woman yelled.

Apparently, the fellow passengers agreed, and they pushed and shoved toward the trolley door. Buster and I scooted between two seats, dragging ourselves across scratchy, prickly glass. A shard pierced my left hand, and I bit my lip to keep from crying out.

What felt like hours later was probably only minutes. The shimmering, tinkling glass settled in a fine layer of dust over everything in the trolley car. Buster stood and brushed himself off, then extended a hand down to me.

"You're bleeding," I said. I reached for his head, and he recoiled. I pulled a lace handkerchief from the wristband of my dress and handed it to him. He took it and dabbed his forehead with it, wincing. We crunched across the mounds of broken glass and stepped down from the trolley into the street.

A crowd had gathered, and all were pointing to the roof of the trolley. I turned, half expecting to see a fiery ball of magma ablaze on top.

Instead it appeared to be part of a huge industrial fan. A group of men leaned out of a shattered factory window nearby.

"Holy blazes!" one of them yelled. "Are you okay?"

The irony of his statement—*holy blazes*—made me giggle in a way that one giggles only when releasing pounds of pent-up anxiety. Not the most appropriate of responses, true.

Our fellow trolley passengers all nodded, inspecting themselves as if they expected to see body parts missing. I pulled the wristband of my dress over the cut in my left hand and pressed it to slow the bleeding.

Buster laughed, then winced and dabbed his wound again. "Coulda peddled some comet pills to that crowd, eh?"

"The pills!" I said. I felt my eyes widen. "How're we going to get them now?" I looked at what was left of our trolley car.

"Hope, are you serious?" Buster tried to wrinkle his brow at me, but instead blinked back pain. "Let's just go home." He cupped his hand about my elbow—which, normally, yes, I would've welcomed—and steered me to the sidewalk.

I jerked my elbow from his cupped hand. "But my Coins—they're counting on me!"

"Coins?" Buster said, then shrugged. "Hope, those pills. They're not real."

I felt flustered, and not just because we'd nearly been crushed by a table-size fan blade. "Don't you see?" I said, looking deep into Buster's brown eyes. "It doesn't matter. *They* think they're real. The Coins. They need those pills. And I'm not going to let them down."

Buster blinked once, twice, then shook his head and smiled. He threw a casual arm about my shoulder, and I thought I might shatter apart and sprinkle about like broken glass.

"I gotta hand it to you, kid. I like 'em stubborn."

Late that evening, close to the turn of the day, Buster and I sold a freshly made batch of pills in our alley. Buster had thankfully remembered to bring a lantern, or the darkness between the buildings might've swallowed us whole.

My Coins were calm once again, now that they had their pills in their clutches. Nathalia gave me a quick hug, then pointed up at the slice of sky peeking between buildings.

Between the smattering of stars, a ball of light the size of Buster's small lantern glowed almost as brightly as the moon.

Behind the ball, a shimmering trail, like a sprinkling of fairy dust, fanned out in a majestic, lopsided crown. It was mysterious and lovely and positively frightening.

"Ain't she gorgeous?" Nathalia breathed. "If I didn't know better, I'd say we've been blessed to witness such a spectacle."

May 16, 1910

TWO DAYS
till the End of the World.

NEWS HEADLINE

Help! Earth Has Design on Comet's Tail!

Two days prior to our lovely little planet tramping through the tail of Halley's Comet, all was business as usual: I performed a trick in which I appeared to be beheaded before a standing-room-only crowd, I sold anti-comet pills to people who needed hope more than money, I avoided any mention of my mother to my father for fear he might implode, and I gave not nearly half of my profits to a snarly little cigar-chomping elf. Everyday stuff.

I was fully prepared to fall into bed that evening and dragged myself up the three flights of sticky stairs at the boardinghouse. But when I rounded the corner out of the stairwell, I saw Cross-Eyed Jane leaning in the doorway of our room.

"Jane, what's—"

Then I saw it. Over Jane's shoulder, I saw the mess that had once been our room. Our mattresses had been stripped and flipped, and they now stood propped against the walls. Our pillows had been sliced open with knives, and feathers still floated about, as if the vandal had just departed. The air smelled like lighter fluid.

Jane's eyes brimmed with tears. "I think they might know about her stash of money, lovey."

They? No, Whitting. I pictured him entering Nick's room, the large ring of keys dangling from the tip of his finger. I hoped with all my might Whitting hadn't returned there.

I stepped into the room, careful to avoid the broken glass vials lying about.

Oh, no!

I stooped and picked up a shard of one of the smashed brown bottles. Its contents spilled on the floor. There were dozens and dozens of them, oozing onto the wooden planks of our room.

Jane's medicines! The vandal had picked the lock on her trunk—on both our trunks—and had busted every single one of the bottles of medicine that Jane sold. Her livelihood was smashed apart and spilling out and stinking up the floor of this disgusting room.

"Oh, Jane." I breathed. My heart felt like it was squeezed by a fist. "I'm sorry."

My trunk was empty, but most of my stuff was lying about. I had moved the money to Nick's room just in time. *Please— please!—don't let him find it there!* I felt sickish at the thought.

Jane's trunk was empty, too. Some of her fake jewels were

strewn over the floor and furniture, but a lot of it appeared to be missing.

"I'm so, so sorry," I choked out again. I wanted to crush the jagged brown vial in my right hand, but all I needed was a cut on that hand, too.

Jane finally stepped inside, careful to step around the puddles of elixirs. "Looks like I'll be taking some time off work, now, don't it?"

Jane wouldn't be able to work without her medicines. And these were *hers*—she paid for them, packaged them, resold them. Without cure-alls to peddle, she couldn't perform. And if she couldn't perform, she'd be fired.

"I'll give you the money to get more," I said, straightening. "This is my fault, and I'll buy you some more—"

"Naw, lovey—hush!" She waved a hand at me, and she seemed more than a little irritated with me. Jane had never, never been irritated with me. "I got money. I'm not gonna take yours.

"It's just gonna take a few days, stockpiling all those things again," she said. "I won't perform for two, maybe three full days."

"The rest of our time in Chicago," I muttered. *Maybe even . . . the rest of our time?*

Jane swept the palms of her hands together, like she was ridding them of dust. "Enough chitchat, lovey. Let's get some brooms and mops from the kitchen downstairs before the house mother sees this mess and gives us the boot."

Two hours later, we'd cleaned most of the mess, though the room still smelled like turpentine, and some parts of the wood floor were now spotty bleached from whatever those bottles contained. I was so tired my eyes burned.

"You ready for bed?" I asked through a yawn.

"Girl, the party is tomorrow night," Jane said. "We gotta fit her one last time!"

Jane had huge black circles under her eyes. But she picked up the lavender dress she'd been altering for me and swiped at some wrinkles.

"Her dress didn't get a bit stained in that ruckus!" Jane smiled, and her eyes leapt about in their sockets. "Fancy that!"

I shook my head but smiled, and slid the dress over my head. The material was smooth silk and felt light and airy on my skin, so unlike the scratchy wool dresses I usually wore. The neckline was wide, not revealing exactly, but it showcased my collarbones in a way that made me feel much older than thirteen. Jane helped me button the line of twenty-some-odd buttons that marched up the back of the dress. The waist swept back into a huge bow that trailed to the hemline. It shimmered and floated when I walked. I felt like an angel, wearing this dress.

I swept in a circle for Jane. She plucked one last pin from the corner of her wrinkled mouth and jabbed it in the hem.

"She looks lovely, she does," Jane said. Her eyes welled with tears again, and I felt so guilty that she was doing all of this for me that I squinched my nose at her. She laughed.

"She can't go making that sour puss at old Benjamin Keith, lovey!" she said.

"That old Benjamin Keith doesn't know whether to scratch his wristwatch or wind his bottom!" I said. Jane howled with laughter, then wiped the corners of her eyes.

"It's missing something, though, love," Jane said, shifting the dress about on my tiny frame. She jerked and tugged, then snapped her fingers.

She shuffled to her trunk, opened it, and popped open a hidden drawer inside. "The vandals don't ever find that secret drawer!" she said, beaming. She held up a brooch, and even in our dim windowless room, the light hopped and bounced off the cluster of gems.

It was a tree, this brooch, with emerald leaves, ruby apples, and a diamond trunk. It was the loveliest piece of jewelry I'd ever seen. "Is it real?" I breathed.

"She bets her sweet feet it's real!" Jane pinned it to the dress, just above my heart. "Every good vaudevillian has a few real ones. Easy to pawn if she's stranded, easy to tote when she's not."

I nodded, but I couldn't say anything. My voice was trapped in my throat. I ran my fingers over that brooch and just kept nodding.

"She's welcome," Jane said, and she gave me a quick hug.

May 17, 1910

ONE DAY

till the End of the World.

NEWS HEADLINE

Comet Parties to Make Chicago Gay Tonight

The day before the possible end of the Earth, the stopping of time, the Ultimate Grande Finale (to which there was no curtain call), I was to go to a fete. A party. A celebration, marking our tiny planet's passage through a potentially deadly comet tail. Of *course,* a party. Right.

The day consisted first of me being handcuffed and submerged in a tank of water. There was little that was more humiliating than wearing bathing clothes onstage. But I survived.

Next, I sold anti-comet pills to an increasingly panicky group of customers. My Coins needed extra pills today, needed extra reassurance. I stayed with them far too long and was late returning to the boardinghouse to get ready for the soiree. I didn't have time to stash my money in Nick's trunk, so

I dumped the quarters into my own. I prayed that Whitting was too dumb to return to my room. But I survived.

I dressed for the party in under ten minutes, despite Bert Savoy insisting on styling my hair. (Cross-Eyed Jane put her foot down on the makeup he thought I needed.) Thank goodness party gloves were in vogue. My fingers bore what might be permanent black stains from constantly touching coins. I donned the creamy white gloves, the lovely lavender dress, the sparkling brooch. I hugged Cross-Eyed Jane, Bert, and Nick good-bye, and cringed as they offered up advice from "Have a dandy time!" (Nick) to "Are you wearing clean skivvies in case of an accident?" (Jane) to "You let me know if that boy acts as anything less than a perfect gentleman" (Bert). I pinched my cheeks and bit my lips to give them a hint of color, and went outside to meet the Three Keatons.

This, I might not survive.

"She's late," Joe Keaton grumbled. Myra laced her arm through his and steered him toward the trolley stop.

"You—wow!" Buster said. I needn't have pinched my cheeks, after all; they burned with blush as his eyes scanned me. I couldn't handle the scrutiny, so I took a sweeping stage bow.

Buster laughed. "You clean up nice, there, kiddo!"

Kiddo. Right. I punched him in the arm, a lean arm covered in a handsome tuxedo. "Ditto."

Buster offered me the same arm, and I cupped my hand into the crook of his elbow. Yowza! If mankind could bottle the kind of sizzle my hand felt just then, electric lights in all the homes would be more than just a dream.

Twenty minutes later, the Keatons and I stepped down from the trolley at the Palmer House Hotel. I had just a moment to crane my neck up the thirteen floors of the redbrick building to glance at the rooftop, where the party would be held.

The gold-and-glass doors swung open, and I was ushered into the lobby. The room was grander than anything I had ever seen: gold gilt carvings at the top of three-story columns. Lush, green plants in planters the size of small automobiles. Purple brocade couches tufted and trimmed with gold cord. Electric lamps and wall sconces. Smooth, satiny wallpaper, between floor-to-ceiling mirrors. It was flashy and gaudy and overwrought—the perfect place to celebrate the demise of our planet.

I know class when I see class. And I'm still looking.

We boarded the elevator, and the operator slid the wrought-iron bars shut across the cage. I'd never ridden on an elevator before. My stomach hadn't, either, and apparently preferred to stay on terra firma, based on the sensation that I'd left it on the ground floor as we shot into the sky.

We reached the rooftop, and the elevator operator rolled the squeaky iron door aside. The cool night air was welcome, and my dizziness disappeared. Maybe a hundred or so round white tables dotted the rooftop. Enormous creations of creamy white lilies and frilly purple irises burst forth from the center of each table. Purple, white, blue, and orange balloons floated every-where. A string quartet played light, airy music—"Shine"—and

I could almost see their tinkly notes lofting toward the heavens, turning into twinkling stars.

Many of the men wore pale blue evening frocks and donned colorful scarves in order to fulfill the request that they adorn the "colors of the firmament." But the women's dresses—oh, my! Sweeping, shifting ghosts of fine fabric, in blues and oranges and reds and purples. Many women wore brooches like mine, but the most stylish women wore bejeweled comets upon their breast—the comet head being a single, impressive diamond, the tail a smattering of smaller clusters.

Talk about swells! These people were so rich, they wouldn't eat ladyfingers unless they were manicured!

I hadn't realized that I had paused at the mouth of the elevator and was drinking in this affair when Mrs. Keaton appeared at my side. "Act like you've seen it all before, honey," she whispered. I nodded but felt a flicker of anger. How did *she* know I'd never been to a party like this before? I could go to one every Thursday, for all she knew.

"Welcome, welcome, y'all!" a Southern voice drawled. She waved our group toward the entrance of the affair. I took her to be Benjamin Keith's wife. "Come on in, get yourself a toddy," she slurred, and held a glass of champagne aloft. "Oh, and here." She flipped open a folded piece of paper with her wrist, and a paper crown popped forth. She crammed one onto my head, then one on Buster's. "Have a comet crown."

The crown was printed on honeycombed paper and bore a large sun in the center, with comets on either side, parading through dark blue skies. Crepe streamers cascaded out behind us. Buster smiled and straightened his crown. "How do I look?" he asked with a lopsided grin.

Adorable. "Ridiculous," I said.

"Really?" He grabbed the lapels of his tuxedo and jerked his jacket from his chest as if to straighten it, too. "Then we're all set. Let's go."

Behind me, I heard Joe Keaton greet Mrs. Keith heartily. "I'll never forget this affair, Bette!" he shouted, and I thought I heard him pound the petite lady on her back. "No matter how hard I try—har, har!"

> *That Joe Keaton. He always enters a room voice-first.*

Our place cards were located at table eighteen, and upon each bread plate sat a party favor: a lovely silver telescope, the size of a thread spool. Engraved in scrolly lettering down the side: *Welcome, Halley's Comet.*

A chill froze me to my core. These people had no fear whatsoever of this comet! Somehow, I supposed, being wealthy made one fearless. I know it would me.

> *The funny thing about money—not only does it make fools out of great people, it makes great people out of fools.*

173

Also lying next to our plate was a pair of paper eyeglasses. "Fan-*tastic!*" I heard Buster yelp, and he looked at me, already sporting the goofy goggles. "You gotta try these, Hope!"

I giggled. Where was Mrs. Keaton now that her son was the one acting up? I folded open the paper glasses and put them on. Every light I looked at—every candle, every star—was cut by the waxed paper in the glasses into the shape of a comet. Dozens of comets, actually, parading before each of my eyes. I shuddered and yanked the glasses off.

"Yes. Amazing," I muttered.

I saw Joe Whitting across the crowd and spun on my heel in the opposite direction. The last thing I wanted at my first formal affair was a confrontation with the gentleman who was blackmailing me. I didn't think he saw me.

The party patrons awaited the rise of the comet, the moment at which the beast broke free from the horizon and danced across the night sky. The evening inched forward, as did Mr. Halley's comet. In the meantime, the partygoers loosened up their tongues with drinks sporting names like Comet Cocktail, Halley's Highball, Nucleus Brandy Cocktail, and the Cyanogen Flip. That last one pained me to hear it, as I remembered how scared my one-time Coin had felt about the possibility of cyanogen poisoning.

And oh, my! The spread! The food buffet had leafy green things and shiny oranges and a huge, bloody roast beef.

Delicious! Until now, I'd thought the only flavor of meat was charcoal!

Buster and I ate two, then three plates, giggling like we were getting away with something sly. I shook my head as Buster popped a cream puff in his mouth, then dropped a handful of puffs in each pocket.

After we'd stuffed ourselves to the point of near sickness, Buster pointed at the dance floor. "Can you place me on your dance card, m'lady?" he said, waggling his eyebrows. I melted a little, but shook my head.

I'm a great dancer, except for two things—my feet!

"You go," I said, and watched him twirl and charm all the older ladies on the dance floor. I sighed, a rare feeling of contentedness about me, and wished that my mother could see me now.

As the evening grew close to midnight, the comet finally peeked above the rooftops and slowly climbed higher and higher into the sky. She dazzled us with her glow—she was as bright as a streetlamp, her skirts a dazzling dusting of light. The whole sky seemed to crackle and fizz. The crowd watched the comet parade across the heavens through opera glasses and field glasses from the War Between the States. Mrs. Keith grabbed an empty champagne bottle and spun about, the air whooshing over the mouth of the vessel. She then corked it again.

"I'm bottling the night air for my grandchildren!" She hiccupped and flipped her wrist about. "Who knows what elements are swimming about us right now!"

Other patrons laughed and followed her lead, collecting and corking the deadly comet air. I realized I was shaking my head.

It felt dangerous, this party. It felt like we, as a collective, were shaking our fists at the skies and yelling, *Is that all you got?*

Before I knew what I was doing, I blurted out, "Aren't any of you afraid of what is to come?"

The party seemed to freeze in time, and all eyes turned to me. We were transfixed, placed under the spell of the comet. I wished I could hop aboard that crazy celestial visitor and ride off into the sky.

I shrugged and smirked and tried to pretend like I had been merely kidding. A few patrons chuckled, welcoming my dismissal of my own statement.

"Don't you try to peddle any of those comet pills to *this* crowd," I heard a gruff voice slur. My heart clutched.

Joe Whitting stumbled forward. He was so besotted, I could almost see the waves of alcohol rising from him. His eyes were two black lines; his cigar chewed to a mealy mush. "These people are far smarter than those rats you peddle your pills to. Don't try to drum up any business with that whole *be afraid* bit. It ain't gonna work here, girl."

That Joe Whitting. He gets worse every day, and today he's acting like it's tomorrow.

My anger crackled and fizzed like the comet just behind my shoulder. Buster tugged my elbow. "Let's go," he whispered.

But before we could melt away, I felt another presence behind me. "Comet pills?" his deep voice bellowed.

I turned and came face-to-chest with a line of gold buttons marching up a purple silk vest. I looked up, up, up and saw a bald head silhouetted against the bright light of Halley's Comet behind him. I couldn't see any facial features, because they were masked in shadows. But I knew who it was.

Benjamin Keith.

"What's this about comet pills?" he asked. I couldn't tell if he was angry or amused, but my heart leapt about in my chest as if it assumed he was cross.

"That's ludicrous!" I heard a light voice laugh. Myra Keaton appeared at Mr. Keith's side and slid her arm through his. "That Joe Whitting—such the imagination. Comet pills!" She threw her head back in an exaggerated laugh. I was surprised that the other patrons did, too.

Joe Whitting scowled and jabbed a finger at me. "No! She does! She sells comet pills! Ask her!"

I held my breath, but the laughter grew the angrier Whitting became. I glanced up at Benjamin Keith and saw his massive shoulders shaking.

"Good one, Joe!" he bellowed. He clamped an arm about the shoulder of his elfin employee. "Comet pills! Wish I'd thought of that a month ago!"

The crowd roared with laughter, and Joe Whitting fumed. Mrs. Keaton flashed a look at Buster and me. *"Go!"* she mouthed, and jerked her head toward the elevator.

We didn't need to be told twice. We left.

Rescued by Myra Keaton.

Nick was right. Miracles *do* happen.

We stumbled out of the garish lobby and onto the sidewalk, and the cool air blasted us. Buster and I looked at each other and burst into laughter.

"I thought you were done!" Buster whooped. "Oh, boy, that Whitting! How long has he known about the pills?"

I told him everything: how I'd been giving Whitting not quite half of my profits, how I'd stashed money in Nick's room, how my room had been ransacked. I did *not* tell him I'd suspected his mother had sold me out. She obviously had not.

Buster rubbed his chin and nodded. "Well, good thing I grabbed these!" He flapped open the jacket of his tuxedo, and three firecrackers were tucked neatly into the breast pocket.

"Let's have a little fun," he said with a wicked lopsided grin. I almost exploded like a firecracker right then.

He looked up at the rooftop. "Now, let's see. I guess we'll need to get onto the roof of one of the nearby buildings. . . ."

"Not at all," I said, pointing to a lovely couple leaving the hotel. They had apparently been at the party, too—they sported crushed comet crowns, wore colorful dresses and amazing jewelry, and they swaggered toward a private coach. They also had balloons.

Buster smiled so big I thought I could see his molars. "Kid, you are good!" I watched as he approached the couple, helped load the tipsy wife into the coach, point at a balloon, point at me, and return with two balloons—one purple, one red—in hand. I imagined him explaining that his lovely date had been highly disappointed leaving without a balloon.

I smiled. "What did you tell them?"

"What? Oh. I told them my kid sister was being a brat and wouldn't leave until she got a balloon."

Hmmph. Not quite the same thing. But then he smiled and winked. I couldn't tell if he was kidding—that he *hadn't* told them that—or if he was softening the blow of being delegated the role of whiny kid sister. Either way, it worked. I huffed a laugh.

We scooted behind the hotel into the alley—a place that felt familiar—and we got to work, knotting the three firecrackers together with the strings of the two balloons. In the dark, quiet alley, the notes of the string quartet playing "Silver Star" dropped down upon us.

Buster drew a pack of matches from his pocket. The box read, PALMER HOUSE HOTEL. He thought of everything! He scratched a match to life. I held the firecrackers while he lit them, and once the wicks were sizzling, he said, "Let go!"

I did, and the balloons wobbled slowly into the sky. I thought at first that the weight of the firecrackers would be too much for the balloons to rise, but then a gust of wind lifted our contraption higher and higher.

We watched our balloons get about ten stories high, and then—

POW! POP! KAPOW!

The blasts echoed off the surrounding buildings and amplified their noise. It was so loud in the alley, Buster and I plugged our ears. I hoped it was just as loud on the roof.

"It's the comet!" a voice shrieked. "The comet has brought forth Judgment Day!"

Buster looked at me with question marks in his eyes. A smile crept across his face. "Was that . . . ?"

I nodded and matched his smile. "The person screaming? Yes, *that* was Joe Whitting."

TODAY

Is the End of the World.

NEWS HEADLINE

Fire Alarms Tell of Comet's Coming

*S*ometime between 11:20 p.m. this evening and 1:20 a.m. in the morning of the 19th day of May, Earth shall pass through the tail of Halley's Comet. Nary a soul knows what to expect.

This thought—or the essence of the thought, at least—permeated my every action on May 18. Nick and I performed a levitating trick, and as I hung suspended in midair (or so it appeared to our audience), I could think of nothing but a comet, suspended in the night sky, barreling toward us with such reckless abandon.

I honestly did not believe that the world would perish in a fiery flash of light in one instant. *No,* I thought, *if the world was to perish, it would be a slow, painful death, one in which we'd choke and gag and blister and burn from the inside out.* I could almost feel the acidic air scalding the delicate tissue of my lungs right then.

See? It was a little difficult, focusing on magic tricks on May 18.

Nick's standing-room-only crowd whistled and whooped as he told us to "suspend our disbelief and *focus*! Drive this comet and its poisonous periphery away with our singular, focused faith!" He was on fire. The crowd wept.

After we took seven, then eight bows, we rushed offstage, and I, straight into Myra Keaton. Nick was already floating out of the building, and Buster and his father entered from the opposite side of the stage, so for the moment, it was just Myra and me.

I had obviously misjudged her, a feeling I was unaccustomed to. "Hey, uh, thank you for last night," I choked out. Had the gasses been eating my lungs already?

"No problem, sugar," she said, and winked a wall of eyelashes at me. "I gotta say, if I ever find a way out of vaudeville, you better believe I'm snagging it, too."

"You're kidding!" I said, and snorted a laugh. Her forehead crinkled. I'd obviously stung her feelings.

Sometimes I need but one thing to make a fool of myself—a chance!

"It's just . . . well, you seem like such a natural at all this," I said. Sheesh. Could this moment be more unbearable?

Myra smirked and clicked her tongue. "Just adapted is all. No, I'd love to leave all this *glamour*. . . ." At that, she swooshed her wrist over the floors slick with goo, the piles of dusty, broken props. "I'd love for Buster to have some kind of a real life," she added in a whisper, her makeuppy eyes lowered to the floor. I didn't know what to say to that, so I remained silent.

"You know his name's not even really Buster?" she asked, her eyes glinting with tears.

"No?" I asked. *What is it?* I ached to shout. But I refrained.

She huffed a sharp laugh. "No. Harry Houdini named him Buster when he was six months old. Fell down a flight of stairs, that kid. Harry said, 'That kid sure can take a buster!' He's been called that ever since. Kinda sealed his fate, that name." Myra looked over my shoulder at Buster, waiting backstage opposite us. He was hopping up and down and stretching, preparing himself for the abuse he was about to endure onstage.

"Poor kid was born in a boardinghouse in Kansas City," she said with a sigh. "He's never known any other life than vaudeville. So sad, don't you think?"

I nodded. Indeed it was.

Buster and I spent every spare moment in the back alley with the Coins on that Last Day. One regular—the redheaded young mother who clutched a small child (and whose name I never learned)—approached me and spoke in an Irish brogue so thick, it sounded as if her tongue had been stung.

"Gerl," she said, gripping my wrist. "Whatever happens tonight, whether theyse pills actually werk, jest know that you've brought comfort to a great many folks."

Her eyes were wide, but not fearful. She'd made peace with

the fact that we must make do with whatever fate was handed to us. I looked over her shoulder, and my other Coins were nodding and smiling.

The mixture of fear and sadness and guilt and—oddly enough—pride that I felt just then bubbled to the surface, and I let out a singular, choking sob. Tears—real ones, not ones that I cried onstage—silently rolled down my cheeks.

Buster placed a warm, strong arm about my shoulders. My Coins—my friends—huddled about me, rubbing my back, smoothing my hair. Funny, but just ten days ago, their crowding me would've made me panic.

Now I didn't know what I'd do without them, every day, from here on.

Around ten-thirty that evening, all citizens in Chicago climbed onto rooftops and into treetops to get the closest possible look at Mr. Halley's fiery beast. Our troupe gathered on the roof of the boardinghouse. Everyone was there but a handful of performers, including Nick, who chose instead to fight for a spot on the shores of Lake Michigan to view the comet. It was a full moon as well, so the evening was bright and crisp, with night shadows scattering about below us, mocking our every move.

Every tick of the clock seemed audible and felt like a leap forward through time, rather than the passing of a mere fraction of a minute. Slowly, slowly, the hands crept about the watch face and dragged us into the eleven o'clock hour.

Buster and I huddled together under a large patchwork quilt that someone in the troupe had dragged to the roof. I still shivered beneath the blanket, and Buster handed me his brown tweed jacket. The arms hung to my knees, and Buster chuckled as I wriggled and wiggled my hands through the mile-long sleeves, piles of extra fabric bunching up my arms.

We drank hot coffee out of tin mugs and laughed while the other performers did handstands, juggled, and told jokes. The opening acts for Mr. Halley, I presumed.

All in all, not a bad way to die.

On rooftops all across the city, people counted down the last ten seconds before 11:20, like one would count down the clock on New Year's Eve:

". . . Five! Four! Three! Two! ONE!"

But when we got to one, no one cheered or sang or kissed. We all froze, inspecting one another, as if we'd expected to disintegrate on the spot. Buster reached out, took my hand, and squeezed it.

"We made it this far, kid!" he whispered with a wink.

"Take *that*, you old comet!" I looked over Buster's shoulder to see Bert Savoy scramble atop a huge storage bin (not an easy task considering his poofy crinolines), lift up the many folds of his dress, drop his frilly bloomers, and wiggle his bare behind to the heavens above.

Laughter exploded across our rooftop, and the Cherry Sisters broke into a rather awful rendition of "Shine on Harvest Moon."

Fire alarms across the city were scheduled to go off at midnight, alerting any citizen of Chicago who might still be indoors (though I couldn't imagine that anyone could be, based on the number of people I saw wandering about) that the best view of the comet was available. As we approached the midnight hour,

185

traveling through the tail of Halley's Comet, we watched with wide-eyed wonder as the comet lifted higher and higher into the nighttime sky.

The comet was almost as big as the full moon, and between the two of them, eleven forty-five p.m. was as bright as late afternoon. The comet and its glorious spray of light covered the entire horizon. It looked like shimmering, sparkling gold. It looked like a dream.

I couldn't help but *feel* Earth traveling through the vast stretches of the universe. We were all very cognizant of our celestial trek just then. We were *in* space. It's easy to forget that when the sun rises in the east every morning and sets in the west at dusk. But here were we, a merry little planet filled with love and hate and laughter and sadness, spinning and swirling through infinite time.

It made me feel small.

And electric. Every hair stood on end, every inch of skin tingled. It felt like the tail of the comet was all over me.

Or maybe it was the excitement of Buster's shoulder next to mine?

"It's glorious." He breathed a soft sigh. His profile was silhouetted against the full moon, his wide eyes reflecting the shimmering comet. I nodded.

CLANGCLANGCLANGCLANGCLANGCLANG-CLANG!!!!

I almost leapt out of my electrified skin, the fire bells sliced through the night sky with such harshness. For a moment, I'd been able to forget that our brilliant visitor was deadly. I remembered now.

Buster threw his hands over his ears. "I can't stand that!" he yelled. "I'm going inside. You coming?" I shook my head. I was going to meet this comet head-on.

"Okay," he said. He lowered his hands from his ears long enough to give me a quick hug. A comet shot up my spine. "See you tomorrow," he said with his lopsided grin.

I smiled in return. "I hope."

The alarms were deafening at first, but I grew used to them and was soon able to tune them out completely. Isn't it amazing how quickly one can adapt to less-than-ideal circumstances?

According to the newspapers, the clanging fire bells were intended to alert citizens to prime comet-viewing times. Apparently, not everyone read the newspaper. For after the horrible ringing began, Chicagoans poured into the cobblestone streets, many bedecked in nightclothes, clutching their pets and their prized worldly possessions. The streets became jammed with pushing hands, snarled faces, and crying babies, all staggering about, puzzled looks on their tired faces.

I was leaning over the edge of the boardinghouse, watching the people jockey for space in the narrow street, when I felt a tap on my shoulder.

"Hopeful!" Nick shouted. I spun to look at him, but instead of his usual, wistful, faraway look, he looked cross. Very, very cross. The bright comet cutting the sky above us accentuated the twists and shadows in his face.

"Can you explain these?" He held out a fist, then unclenched it to reveal seven or eight quarters therein.

Drat. He'd found the stash. I clamped my hands around

his. "Nick! Don't go flashing that kind of money around these people," I said, jerking my head toward our fellow performers.

Nick's eyes blazed. "Whose money is this?"

"It's mine. Ours."

"Where did you get it?"

My instinct was to lie, to make up some story about doing odd jobs for Whitting or some other line of bull. But tomorrow we'd likely have a blue envelope waiting for us, right? No way was Whitting keeping us on tour after all this. So I told Nick I'd been selling anti-comet pills.

"What?" Nick looked sick. He sank to a seated position on the roof of the building and slouched against its ledge. "You? You lied to people and took advantage of them? You cashed in on their fears?"

"No!" I shook my head, my heart racing. Suddenly I could hear those alarm bells ringing again. "No, it wasn't like that. Those people needed my pills. They needed me!"

I took the tin of mints from my pocket and handed them to Nick. He inspected the label that Buster had made, touched a pill to the tip of his tongue. His head drooped, and I could barely hear his next words over the incessant, clanging bells.

"Oh, Hope. What would your mother think?"

Anger swelled in my core like a giant, pulsing ball of fire. I had felt many things toward Nick in the past five years— sadness, guilt, fear, sorrow. But I'd not experienced anger. Until now.

"What would my *mother* think?" I heard my voice rising to an unnatural pitch. "I would think she'd say there isn't much difference between the illusion in selling anti-comet pills and the illusion in performing magic tricks! I would think she'd be proud that I found a way to make some money! To make us secure! To keep us safe!"

And then, like a flash of cosmic light exploding between us, I said it. "We didn't have enough money to save her! We couldn't pay for a doctor, Nick. If anyone would understand the importance of money to keep us safe, I would think it would be you!"

I snatched my pills from his hand and ran down the stairs toward my room.

I had *not* cashed in on fear.

Right?

I threw open the door to my room, expecting to fling myself atop my nasty mattress and scream my guts out while the alarm bells would mask my howls. Instead, there was Cross-Eyed Jane, sitting on the edge of her bed, crying.

"Jane? What's the matter?" I sat next to her.

Her face was a mess of tears, makeup, and snot. She swiped the back of her hand across her nose and snuffled. "I got a blue envelope, lovey."

"What? When?"

"Just now. A few minutes ago. That cowardly Whitting just slid it under the door."

I clenched my fists so tightly, my fingernails cut into the palms of my hands. "You're sure you're fired?" I asked. "It's not just a reprimand of some sort?"

Jane snorted. "Naw, lovey. Takes a look-see."

She handed me an already-soggy slip of paper. It read,

We regret to inform you that,
because of your inability to work
the last two days, your employment
with B. F. Keith's traveling vaudeville
troupe is hereby terminated.

"He fired you after he sabotaged your things," I whispered.

Jane somehow heard me say it, under the still-clanging alarms, and nodded. "Don't know what I'm gonna do without the likes of this crew. They keep me young." She placed an arm about my shoulders. "This girl—*she* keeps me young. I'm gonna miss this girl most of all."

I gave her a long, tight hug, then leapt to my feet.

It was time to find Whitting.

May 19, 1910

TODAY

is the End of the World, Part Two.

NEWS HEADLINE

In Tail of Comet Now, Say Astronomers

Just after midnight, when Earth was still skirting through the trail of this celestial tramp, someone finally told me that Whitting had said he was going to the theater. I raced up the block and into the darkened building.

The benches were empty, soulless, and the ratty curtains hung like giant spiderwebs awaiting their prey. The stage was as black as night. It was so dark, I held my hands out before me. My boot heels clicked and echoed as I walked through the theater toward Whitting's office backstage.

"Whitting?" I said, though it sounded like a shout in this heavy silence. "You here?"

I felt my way along the dark, cracked walls toward backstage. Scurrying sounds—the sounds of rats and other night scavengers—fluttered past my feet. I stumbled over a broken floorboard and crashed to the floor, my cut left hand bracing my fall. Pain shot up my arm.

I finally groped my way to the office and kicked the door open with a bang. "Whitting!" I shouted, hoping to catch him off guard. He wasn't here, though he'd left a lantern burning. I grabbed the lantern and continued my search.

The lantern threw crazy, jumping shadows on the walls. "Whitting?" I asked again. I was just about to give up my search when I heard footsteps above me.

The rooftop. Of course.

The only way to reach the rooftop was by a small metal fire ladder that hung on the side of the building. As I climbed it, I wondered if this was the stupidest thing I'd ever done in my life. I decided that, yes, indeed it was.

The comet and the full moon combined were so bright, it took my eyes a moment to adjust, as if I'd entered a sunny day. Once they did, I saw Whitting, balanced on the ledge of the Orpheum Palace Theatre, hands raised to the sky.

He was a target for the comet, this man standing like a tiny x. One gust of wind, and Whitting would be swept away.

I crept toward him. "Mr. Whitting," I whispered, praying I wouldn't frighten him into making any sudden movements. The ledge was just wider than Whitting's feet; his ankles were at my eye level. "I think you should come down from there, Mr. Whitting."

He pivoted nimbly, and I reached a hand toward him. When he opened his eyes, the black anger that had lived there before was replaced by black fear.

"It's the end," he whispered. "You should ask for forgiveness."

I nodded. "We both should." My hand remained extended, shaking.

He nodded, then laughed—a hollow, empty laugh that chilled me to my core. It caused him to sway on the narrow ledge. He wheeled his arms about and finally regained his balance. I couldn't breathe.

"Come down, Mr. Whitting," I said, motioning gently with my hand like one would toward a puppy or a baby. "The people whose forgiveness you should seek are down here, not up there."

He looked over his shoulder at the comet and appeared to consider that. Then, to my surprise and great relief, he nodded, grasped my black-stained fingers in his, and crept down to the roof of the theater.

I still wore Buster's jacket from earlier this evening—had this really been the same night?—and I took it off and laid it across Whitting's shoulders. The jacket was far too large for him, as it had been for me, and it drooped to his knees. He looked like a child, then—a small, scared bald child.

"Let's get you back to the boardinghouse," I said, pulling his elbow gently. "I think you could use a rest."

The manager at the boardinghouse called a doctor for Whitting. Whitting refused to let the doctor give him a shot until after 1:20 a.m. He mumbled that if we were to die, he wanted to do it with his wits about him. I highly doubted that his wits were still about him, but I asked the doctor to please respect Whitting's wishes. I understood all too well the wishes that people have when they are sick. I only wish my mother had had *any* options. Her wishes weren't hers—they were the ones she was stuck with because my father didn't make enough money to pay for one lousy doctor.

At 1:25 a.m., Whitting received an injection of lithium salts. And then he slept.

Honestly? It looked heavenly, that sleep.

At around two o'clock in the morning, I lay in bed, listening to Cross-Eyed Jane snore. People were still wandering about on the roof above me; I could hear their footsteps. I prayed the roof of this shoddy old place wouldn't collapse, something that hadn't occurred to me until I laid beneath the activity. And wouldn't *that* be ironic—being crushed to death by a party of comet watchers.

For the first time in weeks, I drew in a long, deep breath, one that filled my lungs and swelled my chest. Nothing—no gas burns, no choking, no cooked-on-the-inside sensation. The breath trickled from my nose, and I allowed myself the luxury of three, then four additional deep, filling breaths.

The comet had spared us. We'd be dead by now if she hadn't, correct? Mother Nature had played a trick on us and was likely chuckling at us humans with great mirth, lightning bolts and thunderclaps springing forth from her fingertips in glee. Planet Earth had worked itself into a tizzy. We were expecting the fiery demise of our world; the result was less than a candle snuffed out with wet fingers. All of the restlessness, all of the hoopla, all of the prophesizing, had been for naught.

Or had it?

Couldn't this be an end . . . for me?

We had but one final performance that day in Chicago before we were to pack up our things and prepare for tomorrow's departure. Would we be on that train to Lansing? Or would we find a home here in Chicago? I hadn't seen Nick since last evening, so I had no idea if we'd received a blue envelope, too. And quite frankly, I was still rather angry with my . . . with Nick. Imagine him—judging *me*! When all I was trying to do was help! Even after a long night, my anger still burbled every time I thought of the disappointment in his eyes, in his voice.

I dawdled, choosing not to go to the theater until the last possible moment. I was so cross, I successfully avoided Nick's gaze while we waited for our performance backstage, though I could feel his pleading eyes searching mine. When the orchestra introduced us, I slouched onstage and saw what Nick had in store for us today.

The Disappearing Trick.

Nick performed a few halfhearted preliminary tricks, and the crowd seemed utterly unimpressed. They apparently wanted to know what the Magician had to say, now that we'd traversed the deadly comet's tail and emerged, albeit breathlessly, on the other side.

Finally, it was time for me to disappear. Nick gestured to the six-foot-tall maroon box decorated with gold scrollwork and festooned with massive iron hinges and locks. He opened the door of the prop grandly, displaying the plush black velvet interior. Then he balled a fist and slammed it into each wall of the box, demonstrating the solidity of my cell.

"As stable on the ground on which we still stand. Thankfully," he added with an exaggerated stage wink, and the crowd chuckled at the reference to this newfound stability.

I stepped into the box. Nick smiled at me and whispered, "See you on the other side."

But I wasn't so sure.

Nick closed the door, and in the darkness, I heard him click the wrought-iron locks. The moment I heard those clicks, I crouched and ducked out a tiny door cut into the bottom part of the back panel, below the area Nick had punched. I slid between the curtains and stood behind them as Nick began rotating the box. No one in the audience attributed the rustling curtains to me; they thought they rustled as Nick spun the box.

This trick was far easier to perform now that we were in front of the curtain and not behind it. Behind me, stagehands hammered together the frame of the house that the Three Keatons would use in their bit.

"Well, ladies and gentlemen, we certainly had a close shave today, did we not?" Nick asked the crowd, still spinning the box. I could hear them mumbling and shuffling in response. He brought the twirling box to a rest and began unlocking the massive lock with a giant wrought-iron key.

"Perhaps some of you thought we would all . . ." He paused and flung open the door of the prop. "Disappear!"

The audience gasped and applauded my disappearance. While they clapped, Nick sealed the box shut once again. As he did this, I was supposed to duck through the curtains and crawl back into the box. I had but a handful of seconds.

Shouldn't I just stay here? Couldn't I? I had enough money. I could live with Cross-Eyed Jane. I knew Nick would agree to it. I knew he'd say yes. My dream of stopping—of standing still, of living in one home—could start right now.

I could disappear forever. Never come back.

As I pondered this, I missed my opportunity to leap into the box. Nick began spinning it again, whirling and twirling in tiny, tight loops.

"But we didn't disappear!" Nick bellowed. "We did it, folks! With our collective will, we dissipated those deadly gases! Our faith has saved us, once again!"

He expects me to be there, I thought. *He has faith in me. He's going to open that box, and I'll have disappeared.* My heart sank at the thought of it.

I peeked through the curtains. Nick brought the spinning box to a halt.

He paused then, and I saw it: the spark in his eyes that he gets only when he's performing. My memory flashed: Nick's eyes, sparkling upon my mother, as she lay sick in bed, watching him do some silly little card trick. And my mother, laughing.

She had been happy.

My mother had been happy, and my father missed her. They had loved each other. And I loved them. I reached into my pocket and touched the square of red flannel, the tiny corner of newspaper with Nick's confession.

A home without Nick wouldn't be a home. But a railcar and a boardinghouse and a stage? They could be. Home. With Nick.

I peeked again through the curtain, and realized that Nick had paused too long. He was giving me a second chance.

"Our faith has saved us once again!" he repeated. At the word *faith,* I leapt. I shot through the trapdoor in the box and jumped to my feet just as Nick swung open the massive front door.

I tumbled out of the box, and Nick swept me up in a rare hug. We parted and took deep bows to a wildly applauding audience.

Just as we were about to bound offstage, Nick lifted a single finger in the air. A hush fell over the audience. He smiled.

> When I heard the learn'd astronomer
> When the proofs, the figures, were ranged in
>   columns before me,
> When I was shown the charts and diagrams, to
>   add, divide, and measure them,
> When I sitting heard the astronomer where he
>   lectured with much applause in the lecture-
>   room,
> How soon unaccountable I became, tired and
>   sick,
> Till rising and gliding out I wander'd off by
>   myself,
> In the mystical moist night-air, and from time to
>   time,
> Look'd up in perfect silence at the stars.

Never in my life had I been so happy to hear Walt Whitman.

My own advice to Whitting drummed through my head: *"The people whose forgiveness you should seek are down here, not up there."*

The Coins. Not my mother.

And so I went to the alley behind the Orpheum Palace Theatre and Heel Thy Sole shoe repair. I wheeled my Herkert & Meisel trunk—heavy with noisy quarters that I'd retrieved from Nick's room—with me. Each and every Coin I could find would receive a full refund.

The alley was a dreary, drippy place without my Coins. It was filled with the assaulting smells of garbage and darkness. But I stood in the middle of the alley and I waited.

No one came.

I hadn't really expected them to come. It was May 19th. Everyone on Earth had survived the comet. Not just those who'd been swallowing anti-comet pills. I prayed my Coins didn't hate me. I prayed that they saw false hope as better than no hope.

Never before had I stooped so low. I usually didn't have to—I'm barely four feet tall!

Huck. Those awful wisecracks. I supposed I'd just have to get used to them.

I waited for two full hours, pacing through slop and puddles. Finally, I had to go home.

I found a bent, rusty nail sticking out of a broken two-by-four, and I scratched into the mud where I stood:

I'm sorry.

May 20, 1910

NEWS HEADLINE

Calculations Indicate Tail May Have Passed Earth,
Missing It by 197,000 Miles

Nick and I stood on the train platform, readying ourselves
to board the smoky black train to Lansing. Throngs of
people pushed and shoved around us, and other performers
lollygagged on the platform with us. The stagehands hefted
and loaded our trunks, noting with their thick, black markers the
ones that belonged to performers who'd cheated them on a tip.

I stood on tiptoe, searching the crowd for Buster. It was difficult to discern one man from another, as they all wore similar
wide-rimmed, banded hats. Not a single, lean, tattered-trousered
fellow in the lot.

I hadn't seen Buster since midnight, the night of the comet.
Had the Three Keatons served their time on the small-small-
time circuit? Perhaps they'd been promoted back to the big-time

level of vaudeville they were accustomed to. I took note that I was biting my lip and craning my neck. Not subtle.

Nick reached over and rubbed my back. "I thought we might not be on this train, Hopeful."

I dropped back down to flat feet. "What? Why's that?"

Nick chuckled. "Come, now. Surely you thought we might get a blue envelope on this leg?" His smile was teasingly large.

He had known? I shook my head and grinned.

"Our popularity here was a fluke," he said, and sighed. "Our bag of magic just fit so nicely with the comet."

He looked so sad, him in his knowledge of our fleeting popularity. Nick had loved it, this month of adoration. Of course he had. And I'd been too preoccupied to notice.

"But, we did it, Hopeful," he said, more to himself than to me. "We moved that comet past us with sheer will. We altered the cosmos!"

I knew that Nick thought—no, *believed*—that this was true. And who knows? Maybe we had. Moved that comet. Who truly knows the results of faith?

Nick lifted and dropped his shoulders in a huge sigh, then clapped his hands and rubbed them as if he were washing the dust of Chicago from his palms. "It bought us one more year, that comet. By next year, something else will come along. Right, Hopeful?"

"Right." Personally, I was happy to have that comet travel on its merry way. It was a blessed relief to have fears turn out unfounded, as they so often do not. Thank goodness Halley's Comet would not be seen again with mortal eyes until 1985. Good riddance.

Nick suddenly put one hand on each of my shoulders and lowered his face over the top of my head. It took me by such surprise, this gesture, that I almost backed away.

"I loved her, Hopeful," he whispered into my hair. I absorbed this, rather than heard it.

I nodded, his cheek on my head, and slipped my hand in my pocket to show him I knew this. The scrap of newspaper I'd taken from his trunk remained wrapped in the red flannel quilting square. When Nick saw the fabric, his eyes brimmed with tears, matching mine.

"That's hers?" he said, fingering a corner of the fabric. I smiled and nodded again, a little embarrassed by my choice of keepsake.

He fished a copy of *Leaves of Grass* by Walt Whitman from the breast pocket of his jacket and pulled out the yellow, frayed scrap he used as a bookmark.

"This, too."

I laughed and threw my arms about his waist in the biggest hug I could give.

Nick inhaled and inhaled and inhaled, then bellowed over my head:

I swear the earth shall surely be complete to him
or her who shall be complete.
The earth remains jagged and broken only to him
or her who remains jagged and broken!

More Whitman. I rolled my eyes but grinned, and noticed more than one of our fellow performers standing nearby did the same. Nick loosed himself from our hug, reached in his pocket, grabbed a handful of Sen-Sen mints, and began crunching.

"Stay here, Nick," I said. "I'll be right back."

I had to go tip our stagehands.

As I bent over my trunk, I felt a tap on my shoulder. I nearly leapt out of my skin, but smiled when I saw Cross-Eyed Jane. My eyes swam with tears.

"None of that, lovey," she said, tears welling in her crazy peepers. "The girl should know better than to make a crooked-eye cry! Don't she know tears roll down my back?"

I chortled and grew even tearier.

Jane swiped at the corners of her eyes with the back of her hand. "Just came to say she better pays us a visit when she comes back to Chicago next year."

"You know it," I said. "You going to be okay, Jane?"

"Absolutely!" she said, and flipped her hand at me, dismissing me. Her dozens of bracelets jangled. "This old gal's gonna get herself a job at an apothecary! Me, peddling aspirin! Now ain't that a hoot!" She tossed her head back in a giant lurch of laughter.

"And you're gonna be okay, too, now that Whitting's off the tour, girlie," Jane added. She waggled her eyebrows at me, her wild eyes spinning about.

"Come again?" I said. I felt a smile spread across my face, despite the pity I felt for the man.

"Old Keith said the fella needs a rest. He's taking a 'forced leave of absence.'"

I nodded, then jutted my chin at Jane's trunk. "Did you check out of the boardinghouse?"

Jane kicked her trunk with the side of her foot. "Sure did! No way am I staying in a rat trap like that if I'm not with the rest of the troupe!" We laughed.

"You sure you don't want to hop the train with us?' I asked. "I could use a good soothsayer." I grinned.

She shook her head. "Lovey," she said, and threw her arms about me in an unexpected hug. My eyes filled with tears again.

"She don't need no soothsayer," she whispered into my hair. "She just needs to stay out of trouble. Hear?"

I nodded and blinked back tears.

"Now, watch my things while I go hug her daddy," Jane said, releasing me. She was gone but a moment, hugging Nick, then returned. She squeezed my hand, then tipped her trunk onto a small dolly.

"Lawsy, mercy, this trunk is heavy. I do reckon I am up in years, after all," Cross-Eyed Jane said, and wheeled her trunk away.

Guess I'd learned a thing or two from my old man, after all. Namely, my sleight of hand. Cross-Eyed Jane didn't even notice that while she'd hugged Nick good-bye, I'd hefted all three heaping bags of money into her trunk.

Our bags had been loaded, I'd tipped the stagehands, and I'd given away all the money I'd made in the past month. Our train departed in two minutes. I looked back at the train station one last time, hoping to see Buster's lanky frame striding toward me.

Nothing. I sighed.

"Hey! You coming to Lansing, kid?" I looked up to see Buster in the doorway of the train, one hand gripping the handrail, the rest of his tall frame leaning out over the train platform in a most teasing manner. His smile was as big as I've ever seen it.

I unpinned my traveling hat and strode toward the train car. My mouth puckered sidewise, I was trying so hard not to smile.

"Don't call me kid."

Isn't it a far stronger life if you weaken just a little?

Author's Note

NEWS HEADLINE

Comet Pills: And Other Things Hard to Swallow in the News

Between the hours of 11:20 p.m. on May 18, 1910, and 1:20 a.m. on May 19, 1910, Earth passed through the tail of Halley's Comet. In the days leading up to this, many believed this would be the end of the world, despite constant assurance from world-renowned scientists that no harm would befall Earth's inhabitants. Rumors circulated the globe: The floods in Italy were due to the passing of the comet. One could escape the wrath of the comet by being on or above water (and subsequently, hundreds of citizens stood on bridges and boats during those fateful two hours). The comet was said to carry the plague and influenza germs. Farmers removed lightning rods from atop their barns, fearful they'd attract dangerous substances from the comet's tail. Many farmers so believed the end was near, they didn't plant crops at all.

Anytime there are fears as rampant as these, there are people who cash in on those fears. "Comet-protecting umbrellas" were sold, as were gas masks, protective clothing, and excursions to the moon (payable in advance, of course!). And yes, there really was an enterprising young soul who profited from the sale of comet pills! In Port-au-Prince, Haiti, a medicine man was reported selling "anti-comet pills, guaranteed to stave off all malevolent effects of Mr. Halley's visitor," for a mere $1.00 per pill. (One dollar in 1910 was a lot of money—it could buy a hat, or a dozen eggs, a pound of butter, a pound of cornmeal, *and* a tube of Sanitol toothpaste, or a brand-new invention called a "teddy bear." Hope's pills—which sold for a quarter—were a relative bargain!)

The headlines at the opening of each chapter are original headlines (including the "Comet Pills" one above!). Most are from the month of May 1910 (although I've sometimes tweaked them based on our story—for example, I changed the city from Boston to Chicago.)

Buster Keaton, Bert Savoy, Benjamin Franklin Keith, the Cherry Sisters, and many other vaudevillians featured in this story were real people. Buster was in fact born on the vaudeville circuit and began performing at age three. He and his mother and father—Myra and Joe—really did travel the small-time circuit in 1910 after a controversial tour of England in 1909. (Buster's father, Joe, once wrote in an article for *Variety* magazine that the Three Keatons left England after a single performance, and they were not even allowed the luxury of taking a bow.) Buster stayed on the vaudeville circuit until he was twenty-two. He later went on to Hollywood and starred in many movies, and received an Honorary Academy Award in 1960.

Vaudeville—live, variety theater—was the birth of the entertainment industry in America. It is rich with amazing stories and fantastic personalities and was one of the first true "melting pots" in the world, showcasing performers from any nation, of any color or orientation, so long as they could entertain. Anyone who loves movies or television shows owes a debt of gratitude to these pioneers and their grueling work schedules.

And speaking of vaudeville—the wisecrack jokes Hope "hears" throughout the book were a favorite part of the show for many attendees. Milton Berle and Ed Lowry were two of the most popular one-liner comedians, and many of the jokes sprinkled throughout this text were made famous by them. Many of the jokes are a century old, and they were frequently "traded" across comedians throughout vaudeville.

Halley's Comet traverses near our tiny planet every seventy-five to seventy-six years, passing the planet twice—once on its way toward the sun, in the fall, and once on its way from the sun, in the following spring. I was fourteen when Halley's Comet approached Earth in 1985, and while its arrival was greatly anticipated, the fervor was not nearly that of 1910. My mother woke me one night in the spring of 1986 to watch the comet pass. It was unfortunately unspectacular, as light pollution from streetlights and houses washed out the brilliance of the show in most areas of the United States. What I remember vividly, however, is that the ill-fated space shuttle *Challenger* was on its way to study the comet when it exploded during takeoff on January 28, 1986. It is predicted that the comet will next be visible from Earth in July 2061.

The passing of Earth through the tail of Halley's Comet has been described as the world's first case of mass hysteria. The fear created through the "abundant" media (that is, newspapers—radios weren't yet widely available), combined with the clashing of held-over Victorian sensibilities and Industrial Age objectivity, created a spark that made May 1910 one very interesting month.

ACKNOWLEDGMENTS

A book is a planet, a delicate balance of ecosystems and satellites and a vast universe of support keeping it in orbit. Thank you to the following for their heavenly help:

Linda Ragsdale, who read a handful of pages many moons ago and encouraged me to keep going.

Darcy Maloney, who is an extraordinary first reader and a shining star.

The angels in my critique group—Rae Ann Parker, Jennifer Lambe, and Hannah Dills.

The Chicago Historical Society and the Chicago History Museum, whose online database is stellar. Too, the staff is extremely helpful.

The staff and volunteers in the Society of Children's Book Writers and Illustrators. You keep hope alive.

Josh Adams of Adams Literary, whose support is akin to gravity. Thank you to him, Quinlan Lee, and Tracey Adams.

Liz Szabla, who provided gentle, glowing insight. Many

thanks, too, to Jean Feiwel, Rich Deas, Allison Remcheck, Dave Barrett, Anne Heausler, and all at the star-studded Feiwel and Friends.

My sisters, Cory Grisham and Kathy Goodman, whose orbits are hard to follow.

And to the sunshine in my life: Chloe, Jack, and Byron. Thank you for making every day full of hope.

Recommended Reading

If you're interested in learning more about vaudeville, Halley's Comet, or any of the poets or philosophers quoted in this book, please check out the following:

Albee, Edward F. "Twenty Years of Vaudeville." First appeared in *Variety* September 6, 1923. Vol. 72, No. 3. Found at xroads.virginia. edu/~MA02/easton/vaudeville/albee.html.

"Buster Keaton: American Masters/PBS." Found at pbs.org/wnet/ americanmasters/database/keaton_b.html.

The Chicago Historical Society and the Chicago History Museum. Found at chicagohs.org/research

Etter, Roberta and Schneider, Stuart. *Halley's Comet: Memories of 1910.* Abbeville Press: New York, 1985.

Hakim, Joy. *An Age of Extremes: 1870–1917.* Oxford University Press: New York, 1999.

"The History of Vaudeville." Found at lazervaudeville.com/sghistory .html.

Howells, William Dean. "On Vaudeville." First appeared in *Harper's Monthly Magazine,* April 1903, Volume 106, pp. 311–15. Found at xroads.virginia.edu/~MA02/easton/vaudeville/howells.html.

The International Buster Keaton Society. Found at busterkeaton .com.

Keith, Benjamin Franklin. "The Vogue of Vaudeville." First appeared in *National Magazine,* November 1898, Vol. 9, pp. 146–53. Found at xroads.virginia.edu/~MA02/easton/vaudeville/keith.html.

Kerley, Barbara. Illustrated by Brian Selznick. *Walt Whitman: Words for America.* Scholastic Press: New York, 2004.

Levin, Jonathan, Editor. Illustrated by Jim Burke. *Poetry for Young People: Walt Whitman.* Sterling Publishing: New York, 1997.

Lewis, Robert M., Editor. *From Traveling Show to Vaudeville: Theatrical Spectacle in America, 1830–1910.* The Johns Hopkins University Press: Baltimore, 2003.

Metz, Jerred. *Halley's Comet, 1910: Fire in the Sky.* Singing Bone Press: St. Louis, MO, 1985.

Panati, Charles. *Panati's Parade of Fads, Follies, and Manias: The Origins of Our Most Cherished Obsessions.* HarperPerennial: New York, 1991.

Pendergrast, Tom and Sarah. *UXL American Decades: 1900–1909.* Thompson Gale: Detroit, 2003.

Slide, Anthony. *New York City Vaudeville.* Arcadia Publishing: Charleston, SC, 2006.

Thoreau, Henry David. *Civil Disobedience and Other Essays.* BN Publishing, Chicago, 2009.

Thoreau, Henry David. *Walden, Or, Life in the Woods.* Castle Books, Victoria, British Columbia, 2007.

Whitman, Walt. *Leaves of Grass.* Random House: New York, 1950.